D0008681

Love in ...

Full House –

Miss Black America

Snowflakes – 55-62 mdy

When Did you Stop

Loving Me

HARLEM MOON
BROADWAY

Braiding – important
big day especially

- Grows out of the Black Arts movement
- Images and symbols of real African Americans
- Post Civil right Novel
- Angela's mother Traced out of the Black women working image in U.S.A during 19th century.
- Some Allusions to Images of Post Civil rights Narrative

- Some representations are expressed using food. [Chocolate:]
  - Positive in how it is non-threatening and desirable
  - Negative in that it allows Blacks to be appropriated.
  - Everything but the Burden - Commodify Black Women.

See Black Aesthetic throughout Novel w/ use of influential famous figures. Images were used to Defend Blacks against Stereotypes of Black Life & in embracing Self-defeating notions of themselves.
   ↳ Angela called a liar.

- Chambers shows that Amer had shifted towards multi-culturalism. [7, 42]

- Teddo represents a Black-Hippy — states things and behaves in a counter-culture method. Hippy behavior w/ Black Rhetoric & Dialect. [57, 86-89: Moving to Africa as Black Amer. Esd. selves as expatriates

          • Pg 24

Black Arts Movement : Artist & writers do
abandon symbols & myths that appeared in
European History & Euro-Amer tradition. Instead
use myths & symbols that appeared in the
U.S.A.

- Literary use was for Black Masses not
elite.

- Written by Black Writters

- Portray positive realistic images of
Blacks & Lifes

Also by Veronica Chambers

Mama's Girl
Having It All?

Harlem Moon

Broadway Books

New York

Love in Plain View
Fulleto

Miss Black America

VERONICA CHAMBERS

 A Novel

FOR ANDREA

PUBLISHED BY HARLEM MOON, an imprint of Broadway Books, a division of Random House, Inc.

A hardcover edition of this book was originally published under the title *When Did You Stop Loving Me* in 2004 by Doubleday, a division of Random House, Inc. It is here reprinted by arrangement with Doubleday.

MISS BLACK AMERICA. Copyright © 2004 by Veronica Chambers. All rights reserved. No part of this book may be reproduced or transmitted in any form or by any means, electronic or mechanical, including photocopying, recording, or by any information storage and retrieval system, without written permission from the publisher. For information, address: Broadway Books, a division of Random House, Inc.

PRINTED IN THE UNITED STATES OF AMERICA

HARLEM MOON, BROADWAY BOOKS and the HARLEM MOON logo, depicting a moon and a woman, are trademarks of Random House, Inc. The figure in the Harlem Moon logo is inspired by a graphic design by Aaron Douglas (1899–1979).

Visit our website at www.harlemmoon.com

First Harlem Moon trade paperback edition published 2005

Book design by Dana Leigh Treglia

Illustrated by John W. Mosley

"It's Only a Paper Moon" by Billy Rose, E. Y. Harburg, and Harold Arlen © 1933 (Renewed) Warner Bros. Inc. Rights for the extended renewal term in the United States controlled by Gloria Morra Music, Chappell & Co. & SA Music. All rights reserved. Used by permission. Warner Bros. Publications U.S. Inc., Miami, FL 33014.

"Lift Every Voice and Sing" (written by J. Rosamond Johnson, James Weldon Johnson). Used by permission of Edward B. Marks Music Company.

The Library of Congress has cataloged the hardcover as:
Chambers, Veronica.
    When did you stop loving me : a novel / Veronica Chambers.
      p. cm.
      1. African American girls—Fiction.   2. African American families—Fiction.   3. Bronx (New York, N.Y.)—Fiction.   4. Fathers and daughters—Fiction.   5. Maternal deprivation—Fiction.   6. Motherless families—Fiction.   7. Runaway wives—Fiction.   I. Title.
    PS3553.H2634W47 2004
    813'.54—dc22

                                        2003065396

ISBN 0-7679-1467-8

10 9 8 7 6 5 4 3 2 1

Say it's only a paper moon,
Sailing over a cardboard sea,
But it wouldn't be make believe,
If you believed in me.

—Billy Rose and E. Y. Harburg

Love in Plain View

It was 1979

and escape was heavy in the air. Assata Shakur made a daring bust out of a maximum-security prison. And although my father and I did not yet know it, Mother had also been tunneling her way to freedom. Assata broke out of the Clinton Correctional Facility, guns blazing and motors running, Jesse

James–style. No Cleopatra Jones, mine wasn't a gun-toting mama, though she was the baddest one-chick hit squad to ever break my heart. My mother's getaway was as subtle and silent as a magic trick. She simply walked out the door one wintery evening and never came home. My father was a magician, but my mother was the real Houdini.

It was not the way I understood grief, the way my father and I responded to the shock of it all. Time moved quickly that year and the day she disappeared began to fade from me. A few months after she was gone, I struggled to remember the details of the last day I saw her. What was I wearing? What did I have for lunch that day? What was the last thing she said? Was it "Good-bye, sweetheart, be good." Or was it "Gotta run, baby. Be good." I remembered the "be good," although by the time she was gone for a year, I hadn't been good at all.

In my mind, my mother's face fills every empty frame. Have you seen her? Melanie Aisha Brown. She is five feet ten inches tall. I do not know what she weighs. She wears a size 6 dress and a size 7 shoe. She has dark skin, and straight hair, which she wears in a flip. She is beautiful, look-twice-on-the-street gorgeous. She is thirty-four years old, but can pass for much younger. She likes burgundy lipstick and bright nail polish and anything made from potatoes: potato chips, mashed potatoes, french fries. She smokes when my father isn't around and keeps a pack of cigarettes and a lighter, covered by tampons, in a brown-and-white plastic cosmetics case in her purse. She is a woman with secrets.

♦

When I was six, my grandmother died. I woke that morning to Mommy's screams punctuating the air. All I heard was holler, holler, holler, holler, holler, holler—precise and almost musical, like a church bell, pealing off the hour. I ran into the room and she was in a long pink cotton nightgown that was washed so many times it lost its pattern. Sponge rollers, half undone, hung around her head like a Halloween hat. She nearly wrenched my arm off when she spotted me by the door, pulled me to her so fiercely, as if she feared we were both headed for our doom. Of all the things I have forgotten in the years since Mommy left, this stays with me: her loss, shiny and heavy with heartbreak.

"I have no mother," she mewled in my ear, "I have no mother." I can hear her say it even now, and her voice, as it was then, is low, eerie, haunting, as if the loss was far from singular, but multiple and perpetual. A curse that will haunt woman upon woman in our family line until kingdom come. Which, of course, it will. Eventually.

The day Mommy disappeared, I did not scream as I should have. The day was too much like any other. I came home from school and Mommy wasn't there. My father sat at the kitchen table, eating an omelet and reading the *Amsterdam News*. I remember a riddle my father used to ask. "What's black and white and read all over?" And the answer, not a newspaper, not any old newspaper, but this special one: the *Amsterdam News*.

I asked for my mom and my father told me she was working the night shift at the bank. She cleaned office buildings and sometimes she worked days, 6 a.m. to 1 p.m., but she preferred nights. Fewer people in her way, she said, and I knew that was her pride talking. She dressed to the nines to go to work. Her hair pressed and curled, a gold cross nestled in the bosom of her purple-and-black-striped wraparound dress, high-heeled boots that grazed her knees. She was the proud owner of three of those wrap dresses, each paid for on layaway, and she wore them with the kind of love that only comes when you buy something, as she called it, "on time."

Mommy's eyes were heavy-lidded and almond-shaped; it gave her a sleepy look that men seemed to like. Her half of the medicine cabinet was filled with makeup from Revlon's Polished Amber line. The packages resonated with their slogan: "Now, you don't have to borrow anyone's beauty." Mommy ripped out the ads from *Essence* magazine, pictures of thin, beautiful, brown-skinned women, like Barbies dipped in chocolate. She read the fine print, buying each product to re-create the model's image and practicing a look before wearing it out for the evening. During the day, she wore amaretto nail polish that matched her amaretto lipstick and in the evenings spiced it up with a deep burgundy color called cognac. When she went out with my father, she tucked a fake tortoiseshell compact of pressed powder, with a label that read "Love Pat," in her purse.

Mommy was beautiful and worked hard to radiate beauty, studying the very psychology of the thing. But she only primped in the privacy of our home. "It's not true that beautiful women spend all day at the mirror," Mommy once told me. "It's the exact opposite. It's insecure women who can't pass a mirror without sneaking a peek." She said that even women who had it going on—banging hair, slamming body, the finest clothes—still crept around like Cinderella with one eye on the clock. She said that women who are born into their glory know that the mirror's not a newspaper, it can only tell them what they already know.

When I was with Mommy, people often asked if she was a model or an actress. She did not tell them what she really did for a living. Instead, she smiled broadly, sometimes reaching out to touch the compliment giver on the shoulder, saying "I often hear that." I never went to Mommy's job, but she told me enough about it for me to know what she liked and didn't like. The employee entrance of the bank had a solid door. Mommy liked the bank's front door. "It's all glass," she explained. "And it goes round and round like a carousel." She hated hanging her clothes in a small, dim locker room and exchanging them for the awful pink smock with the embroidered logo of the cleaning company. The itchy pants that she said "Aunt Jemima'ed" her hips, instead of showing them off. And the real punishment—having to pull back her hair.

"Did she leave a note?" I asked, when my father told me Mommy was at work. She usually left me a note on the kitchen table when she worked nights. Her notes told me what to have for a snack, what to warm up for dinner, with the unnecessary reminder to do my homework and not to turn on the TV until I was finished. Each note ended with the same declaration, "I love you, Angela Davis Brown."

"She was running late," my father said, not glancing over his newspaper. "No note."

"Well, I'm hungry. What should I eat?" I asked.

"Whatever you want," he said. This should have been my first clue that something was wrong. My father was always happy to offer an opinion on anything, from politics to popcorn. But I didn't catch it, then. I simply took a couple of chocolate chip cookies from the pantry and went off to do my homework.

♦

That night, when I went to sleep, I found Mommy's wedding picture underneath my pillow. That should have been my second clue, but I didn't know that I was looking for clues. All I thought was, "This is what she left me. She was running late. But this is my note."

The next morning when Mommy didn't wake me up for school, I knew something was wrong.

I panicked, shaking my father who slept alone in his bed. "I'm late for school!"

"So don't go," was all my father said, rolling to face the wall.

"Where's Mommy?" I wailed.

"Something's come up. Your aunt Mona in Chicago is sick. Your mother went to see her."

I was looking for clues then and my father gave me my first one. Mommy hated my Aunt Mona. She spoke to her once a year at Christmas, the annual call prefaced by the exact same comment, without fail: "Family is family. No matter how much of a bitch Mona is."

I shook my father's shoulder until he finally sat up in bed. "Where's my note? Mommy didn't go all the way to Chicago without leaving me a note."

My father started lying in earnest then; his easy manner and flawless delivery told me they were lies. "She left straight from work, Angie," he said, using the nickname we all hated. "Your Aunt Mona has to have an operation. Apparently, there's something wrong with her liver . . ."

I left him, mid-lie, and walked back to my room. I closed the door and began to tear the place apart. There must be a note. There must be an explanation. I looked underneath the bed and under the mattress. I pulled out every pocket of my pants as well as my spring and winter coats. I rifled through my underwear drawer and was about to begin with socks when I saw it: Mommy's straightening comb, wrapped in a brown silk scarf. Mommy was gone. She had left me her comb. I put the wedding photo underneath the straightening comb, then I closed the drawer carefully, so my father did not see my discovered treasures. Then I lay across my bed and began to cry without shame.

♦

Two months before my mother left, I entered the sixth grade. My classroom was decorated with faded pictures of rosy-cheeked white kids with blond hair. These children did not look like any of the cocoa-faced kids I sat in class with. Every conceivable surface—the bulletin boards, the wall above the chalkboard, the wood closet doors—was covered with the illustrated adventures of Dick and Jane. The pictures didn't even resemble the only white girl in our class, Brenda. Her hair was red, just like the comic book character Brenda Starr. She swore up and down that she wasn't named after a stupid comic strip, but that's what all the kids called her, Brenda Starr.

Our teacher was a middle-aged white woman from Long Island. She told us that the very first day of school. "My name is Mrs. Newhouse and I'm from Long Island." She pronounced "Long Island" in a really funny way, as if the word were chopped up into five or six squeaky syllables. I thought it strange that she mentioned where she was from. It wasn't as if Long Island was as interesting a place as France or India.

My fifth-grade teacher at Martin Luther King Jr. Elementary had been Mrs. Chong. She was Cuban Chinese. We only found out about the Cuban part when some of the Puerto Rican kids in class were making fun of her eyes and she went off on them in Spanish. We thought of her clipped, staccato tone as the way all Chinese people spoke. But when she started speaking Spanish, she was like Nydia Velasquez's grandmother, hanging out of the family's second-floor window, cursing people out, neck wobbling. In class, Mrs. Chong put her hand on her hip and one finger in the air and let loose a string of Spanish words that swiveled in her mouth. She was like a comic book hero throwing off her civilian guise to reveal her super powers. We knew then that she was the coolest teacher we'd ever have.

Mrs. Chong explained that her parents were Chinese, but she'd grown up in Cuba. "You better watch out," the boys called out, as they roughhoused in the playground. "Mrs. Chong will do a Bruce Lee on your ass. Then she'll turn around and pow pow like Roberto

Duran." Me and my girlfriends were more concerned with what Mrs. Chong had cooking in her pot. "Her kids must be so lucky," Coco Garcia said, biting into her peanut butter sandwich. "They can have sweet and sour pork one night and ropa vieja the next." Kenya Moore added, "They could have wonton soup and black bean soup." Brenda Starr waved away all comparisons with an impressive air of cool. "Face it," she said, crossing her legs and swinging the top one lazily, "her kids have got it made."

What was so special about a teacher from Long Island compared to a Cuban Chinese? Mrs. Newhouse went around the room and asked every kid what their father did for a living. When she got to me, I said, "Magician." Everyone in the class giggled. Hard of hearing or just not paying attention, she said, "Does your father play an instrument, dear?" I just shook my head. "No, Mrs. Newhouse," I said, "he's a magician." I made the word long and squeaky like her "Long Island" so maybe she'd understand me better.

She smiled at me, a fake smile without teeth, then came over to my desk. She smelled of coffee and, on closer inspection, her red pantsuit was peppered with balls of lint along the thighs. She patted me on the head. "Here's an example of a very vivid imagination at work," she said. "I bet every little boy or girl wishes their father were a magician or a circus ringmaster or a flame eater." She chuckled, as if she'd told a very funny joke.

I didn't say another word the whole day. I just sat there, silent and furious. Because, the thing is, I'd already come to school that day feeling bad. The night before, my mother and father had a huge fight because there was no money to buy me a new outfit for school, much less a pencil case or a small pair of plastic scissors or any of the school supplies on the list the counselor provided us with when Mommy registered me for that new school. This, the issue of no money, I was led to believe, was my father's fault.

Just the night before, Mommy began yelling about how my father was "no better than a child." She stood in the living room wearing a blue-and-green tie-dyed T-shirt and a pair of white jeans. Mad as she was, she was beautiful. I thought she looked like a black Charlie's Angel. Her shoulder-length hair was pressed to bone-straightness, and she wore it flipped back like Jayne Kennedy.

"Some sort of magician you are, Teddo," she screamed, ripping up copies of my father's head shot. "Why don't you pull some motherfucking food out of your hat? Why don't you make some money appear, Magic Man?"

My father closed the paper he was reading, then walked over to the stereo. "You are so small-minded," he said, clamping the bulky headset over his ears. "You've got such a fucking small mind. Can't you see that I'm trying to do something amazing with my life?"

Mommy was on him in ten seconds. She ripped two buttons off his silk print shirt and began pounding on his chest. "Amazing? You want to do something amazing?" she screamed. "Provide for your fucking child. Live up to your fucking responsibilities." He shrugged her off with one strong swoop of his arms. "This is a new shirt, man," he muttered.

Mommy stumbled from my father's shoving, but quickly got to her feet. She cut her eyes at my father, tossing him a long, hard glare, the kind that was an invitation to rumble on any street corner in the city. My father refused to take the bait, humming along to music only he could hear. "Come on, Angela," Mommy said, leading me out of the living room. My hand felt small in hers, and in her anger, her long nails dug deep into my palm. I didn't care.

We were living in the South Bronx, in a former bachelor's pad with love beads and shag carpeting in every room. Even the bathroom was carpeted. As we walked back toward my tiny bedroom, I squeezed the blue shag carpet with my toes. This was the first time I did not have a new dress for the first day of school. I understood the reason, but that didn't hold back the tears. There was no money. Money was often tight, but it had not bothered me before. Now I felt caught. For the first time ever I was drafted into the vicious financial war my parents constantly fought. It felt terrible.

By the time we reached my room, I was quietly sobbing. I sat on the bed and Mommy knelt in front of me. Her dark chocolate face glistened around the edges, like a halo, where she'd combed her baby hair down with Vaseline. She pulled my face close to hers, our lips close enough to kiss, and she said, "I am so sorry. There's nothing I hate more than to see you go without. But I had no choice this month. Either I bought clothes or paid the rent. I couldn't have us out on the street."

The notion of being out on the street was no idle threat. All around our Bronx neighborhood, there was evidence of eviction—sofas, like new, abandoned on the sidewalk; dining room tables left behind when somebody took all the chairs. Sometimes, after it rained, I saw family photographs and copies of birth certificates floating toward the gutter, like paper sailboats sinking into a watery grave.

Mommy grew up running from bill collectors and the repo man. Once, she and my Aunt Mona were in the middle of watching a favorite show—*Laugh-In*—when the bell rang and a guy came in and took the TV. One day, she came home from school and found all of the contents of her apartment on the sidewalk and the neighbors making off with all of her stuff—her dolls, her clothes, even a bag of her barrettes. "Girls I knew," Mommy said, her teeth clenched as if those stolen baby dolls had been real babies. "Girls who had visited my house, played with my toys, just took them. Without four walls around it, your stuff is just not your stuff. I never want you to go through that. Never."

I cried greedy new-dress tears, then Mommy stood and opened my closet door. "It's a brand-new school, Angela," she said in a cheerleader's voice that I didn't believe. "Nobody's ever seen any of your clothes. Just make do for now, sweetie. First of the month, I'll buy you a new dress and new shoes."

I didn't want to hear it and looked away at the poster on my wall of Angela Davis. Her bright brown eyes were flashing and her lips were slightly open, but serious, as if she was in the midst of saying something powerful. I knew what Angela Davis thought of little girls who cried for new clothes—trifling. I quickly wiped my tears and hugged Mommy around the waist.

"Pick a dress," she said, kissing me on the forehead. "I'll iron it and it will look like new, I swear."

I stood up and reached for the outfit we both knew I'd go for: a pink peasant blouse with a pair of pink bell-bottoms to match.

In the kitchen, Mommy gave me a purple notebook with stars and a new purple pen. "No book bag yet," she said.

♦

I hadn't slept well the night before I met my new teacher, Mrs. Newhouse from Long Island. I'd been feeling small and she made me feel smaller. So since she'd already said I was a liar, I went home and I told a lie.

Daddy was in the kitchen, making an omelet. Three o'clock and he was still in his pajamas, which meant he didn't have a show that night, which meant there was no work.

"How was your first day of school, princess?" he asked, sweetly, which told me he was sorry for fighting with Mommy the night before. When Daddy was feeling guilty, there was sweet talk to spare. He'd be calling Mommy "Miss Black America" and his "brown sugar honey dip" as soon as she got home. He would fix dinner, omelets and green salads. I would go to bed early, Daddy would light candles and put on Teddy Pendergrass as soon as I went to bed. I knew the drill.

"Terrible," I said, pouting for effect. "Not to mention, the teacher was talking about you."

"About me?" Daddy asked, whipping around from the hot stove. "What did she say about me?"

For all his skillful hustling, Daddy was easier to play than a game of three-card monte. All you had to do was make him the star of the story, good or bad, and he got right involved.

"The teacher asked us what our fathers did for a living," I said, pausing dramatically. "And when I told her that my father was a magician, she rolled her eyes. She said, 'There's no such thing as a black magician.'"

"She said what?" Daddy growled ferociously. I thought about pretending she'd said that there was no such thing as a nigger magician, but I knew that was laying it on a bit thick. Always keep your con simple.

"She said she'd never heard of a black magician," I repeated. "Then she asked me if I didn't mean musician and she asked me what instrument you played."

"Why we always got to sing and dance?" he fumed. "It's not enough to be a talent like Bojangles!" He stalked back and forth across the tiny kitchen, shaking his head and muttering, "Got to sing 'Good Ship Lollipop' with Shirley Temple." Then he turned to me and grabbed my shoulder. "Angela, you listen to me! It's not a 'good' ship unless white people are on it. Frank Sinatra and Dean Martin hanging out are just a couple of nice guys. Put a black man in with them and all of a sudden, it's the Rat Pack. Always got to be something negative with black people."

"Daddy, the stove," I said, pulling my shoulder from his grip as the skillet began to smoke.

"In the cowboy films, the good guy wears white and the bad guy wears black."

"Daddy! Your omelet's burning."

He turned around and turned off the flame. "So because it's black, I'm not supposed to eat it?" He ate every last burned bite.

◆

The next day, Daddy walked me to school. Although it was only eight o'clock in the morning, he was dressed in a black tuxedo, complete with top hat and tails. I felt silly walking down the street with him. People peeked out of doorways and stared from windows. But I was more happy than embarrassed because I knew that my teacher was going to get it. Daddy was going to give her a tongue-lashing she'd never forget.

Which is exactly what he didn't do. After introducing himself to Mrs. Newhouse, Daddy said, "I understand that this is Career Day at the school."

Mrs. Newhouse, dressed in a teal pantsuit identical to the one she'd worn the day before, went slightly green herself. "I'm afraid there's been a mistake. Today is not Career Day."

"Really?" Daddy said, shooting me a quizzical look. "That's what Angela told me." I was seated in the fifth seat of the third row and although I silently chanted "Abracadabra" neither I nor my chair disappeared.

"Well," Daddy said cheerfully. "Since I came all this way, would you mind terribly if I showed the kids some tricks?"

All the students began to clap. Three or four of the girls, the ones that I'd already designated as the snotty bunch, shot me winning smiles. These were sweet smiles, ripe with the promise of future invitations. I ignored them, unsure that Daddy's spell would last past the minute he walked out the door.

"Actually, Mr. Brown, I'm afraid we don't have time for magic tricks," Mrs. Newhouse said, reaching out for a folder on her desk. "The Board of Ed has laid out a very strict lesson plan. Lots of learning to do, you know." She said this last sentence with a bit of a jump, like a character in a musical.

Daddy clasped his hands behind his back and rocked back and forth on his heels, a "Golly, gee" gesture that he'd stolen from Bob Denver of *Gilligan's Island*, beguiled innocence being a hard look for a six-foot-tall black man to fake. "I won't argue with that," he said brightly. "My great-grandfather always told me that if you pour your wealth into your head, you will always be rich."

Mrs. Newhouse smiled, tight-lipped, and looked pointedly at the door. Daddy began to walk away, then turned around. "My dear Mrs. Newhouse," he said, in a faint British accent designed to flatter. "I need to use the pay phone on my way out. A smart teacher like you, with a head full of knowledge, could probably spare some change." Daddy reached his arm around Mrs. Newhouse's head, just past her modified beehive, then he pulled a quarter out of her ear and she gave a little gasp. The kids in class sat on the edge of their seats. She'd asked Daddy to leave, she'd said there was no time for tricks, but he'd gone ahead and whipped a little something on the teacher anyway.

Daddy lifted a large "Reading Is Fundamental" coffee cup off of her desk and held it up to Mrs. Newhouse's head. "You've poured so much knowledge, so much *wealth*, into your head, that you're a positive gold mine." He did the slot machine trick then, cranking Mrs. Newhouse's arm up and down as quarter after quarter fell out of her ear and into the cup.

The kids began to cheer and even Mrs. Newhouse let loose a giggle. "I have to say," she said, in a whispery tone that bordered on flirtatious, "that is really astounding. Perhaps we can all learn something about magic as part of our lesson plan today."

Daddy took out a large envelope, five notebook-sized playing cards, and a piece of black photographic paper. He displayed each card slowly. On one card there was a plus symbol; on another card there was a square; on the third card there was a circle; on the fourth card there was a series of wavy lines; and on the last card there was a star.

He turned his back to the class and asked Mrs. Newhouse to shuffle the cards. She did and handed the large cards back to Daddy, carefully with two hands as if she was afraid they might fall.

Daddy smiled at the class. "Since I'm taking up some of your important class time, I thought we'd do a review of basic mathematics."

He knelt down and placed three cards facedown on the floor, then he asked, "Ladies and gentlemen, how many cards on the floor?"

Everyone cried out, "Three!"

He stood up again. "That leaves how many cards in my hand?"

All the kids shouted out, "Two!"

"Now what I'm about to show you moves out of the realm of math and into the realm of physics," Daddy continued. His smile glowed as if he was born to bring and experience joy. I sat at my desk, remembering his fight with Mommy two nights before—the way he'd shrugged her off like a fly that bothered him. His face then was so cold, so disgusted. "He is a million men," I thought.

"This, ladies and gentlemen, is what we call mind over matter," Daddy began. He said that kids loved to be called ladies and gentlemen. It made them feel grown-up and was just a little bit distracting, which was good, and kept their minds off the mechanics of the trick. "I'm going to put these two cards face to face and put this magical black photographic paper between them. I'm going to place the whole thing in this envelope and then I want the lovely Mrs. Newhouse to take the envelope to the other side of the room."

Mrs. Newhouse took the envelope and practically skipped over to the little library in the back of the room.

"Now you won't believe what you're about to see," Daddy said. "A year from now, you may not even remember exactly what you saw. But I want you to remember this—mind over matter."

Daddy took off his long tuxedo coat and rolled up his sleeves. He closed his eyes and placed a finger on each temple. Then he began to hum. A few moments later, he announced, "I'm in harmony with those cards. It doesn't matter what they were when I put them in because I imprinted my will on that photographic paper. I have changed the cards!"

In a confident slow-motion stroll, Daddy began to walk up and down the aisles between our desks. He looked each child in the face, pausing suspiciously to gaze longer at certain kids. When he'd made eye contact with every student in the room, including me, he asked, "How many of you believe that I can guess which two cards Mrs. Newhouse is holding in her hand?"

About half the kids held up their hands. "This is a tough crowd, Angela," Daddy said, winking at me. Then he asked for a show of hands again.

He walked over to a boy sitting in the very last row. The biggest kid in the room, he seemed genetically programmed to be the class bully. "What's your name, son?" Daddy asked.

Charlie told him.

Daddy perched on the edge of Charlie's desk. "You don't believe I can guess those two cards," he said.

"Nope," Charlie answered.

"Well, how about I make you a deal?" Daddy purred. "I'm going to take a guess and if I'm wrong, I'll kill myself."

Mrs. Newhouse looked horrified. But Daddy wasn't finished.

He stood up and as he walked toward the front of the classroom, he added, "However, if I kill myself, I'll do it by starvation." He winked at Charlie. "I don't know if you'll want to wait around."

Everybody laughed. Mrs. Newhouse let out a sigh of relief. Then Daddy pronounced, "You are holding the square and the wavy lines, Mrs. Newhouse."

And of course, she was. House rules. The con man always wins. Daddy performed until the lunch bell rang. When he took his final bow, the entire class stood up and clapped until Mrs. Newhouse made them stop.

In the cafeteria, I was surrounded by kids. Not just the ones in my class, but fifth and sixth graders who'd been hearing about Daddy's magic act. They asked a million questions, questions that just begged for me to lie some more. For the first time, it looked like I might actually be popular—old clothes and all. They wanted to know if I'd ever met Doug Henning. I said yes. They wanted to know if we kept a magic carpet at home. I said yes. They wanted to know if we owned a magic rabbit. I said yes. They asked if I knew the secrets behind Daddy's tricks. "Of course," I said, feigning boredom. The truth was I knew some of the devices: hidden compartments, rubber thumbs big enough to squeeze handkerchiefs in, dummy hats and newspapers that were quickly swapped for the real thing. But I couldn't do magic—not even a simple "pick a card, any card" deck trick.

"What's a deck of cards?" my father once asked me.

"Pieces of thick paper with pictures on it," I answered.

He shook his head. "See, that's where you're wrong. We're a nation of gamblers, baby. Everybody wants something for nothing. Even fine, upstanding people want a little more in exchange for a little less."

He shuffled a deck and a flurry of cards flew from his right hand to his left.

Then he put the deck down and picked up one card.

"What's this?" he said, showing me the deck.

"Jack of spades," I answered.

He shook his head again. "It's a lottery ticket, Angela. A deck of cards is fifty-two lottery tickets and the game is easy. The audience bets on you. Ninety-nine percent of the time they're going to bet against you because they're full of doubt. That's okay though, because you have to bet against the house if you're going to win big."

"Huh?"

My father just grinned. "Don't worry about it. You're years away from learning how to bet on the ponies. Just remember, the audience is betting against you. But if you're a good magician, the audience always loses and they go home feeling as if they won."

I looked around at the kids from school, the ones who adored my father and thought they might like me. I wanted to tell them, It's more complicated than you think. Sure, it helps to be a magician's daughter. I've got a few ins. But let's say your mother is Patti LaBelle and because you're her daughter, you can carry a tune. You have to do more than sing. You have to wear those crazy outfits and sport that fabulous hair. You have to know how to dance and how to work an audience. You have to know how to banter and how to wink and how to make a room hot when everyone is just sitting there, staring, as frozen as a glass of ice cubes. You have to be fearless and larger than life. Your mama could be Patti LaBelle, Angela Bofill, and Stephanie Mills all rolled up into one, but unless you can bring the funk, you're just another church mouse singing in the Sunday choir. It's like that with magicians, I wanted to say to all those kids who wanted, for a few days anyway, to be my friend. The tricks are the easy part. All the things my father does that make him amazing? The walk and the banter, the dreams and the madness. That's the real magic.

◆

My mother wielded her own charms. As a very young girl, not more than five or six, I remember Mommy taking me to matinee screenings of *Cleopatra Jones*, *Coffy*, and *Friday Foster*. Pam Grier starred in more movies, but Tamara Dobson, who played Cleopatra, was Mommy's favorite. Cleopatra Jones films were set in exotic foreign locations, her sports car concealed a repository of weapons, her wardrobe was strictly Paris runway. She was black, beautiful, and Bond. Every time we left the theater, Mommy was as wide-eyed and wistful as a little girl. Wasn't Cleo beautiful? Had I ever seen a car so sleek or a woman so brave? Mommy expertly glued on false eyelashes like Cleo's, scoured the flea markets in the West Village for similarly stylish clothes.

My mother had not been born rich and my father asked her how she could miss what she never had. But Mommy taught herself the intricacies of wealth and she missed not having it, every day she spent under Daddy's roof. We spent entire Saturdays in Saks Fifth Avenue trying on clothes that she could never afford. Mommy was good at pretending to have money. More than twenty years later I still jump when an uppity saleswoman yawns a disdainful "May I help you?" Mommy recognized their snobbiness, but she couldn't be beat at feigning haughtiness and entitlement. On the days Mommy went pretend-shopping, she did not leave the house unless she was freshly showered and dressed in one of her favorite wrap dresses—no makeup, lest it get on the clothes. She also read the paper before each expedition.

The saleswoman we encountered one rainy Saturday afternoon, at Saks, was six feet tall, blond and forty-something. She was dressed head to toe in a V-neck black silk blouse and black palazzo pants that draped her nonexistent hips expensively. There was no hint of the service gene in the woman's "May I help you?" Mommy answered crisply, "Yes, I need something to wear to the opera." As the woman pulled clothes from the rack she oh-so-casually asked what Mommy was going to see. Having done her homework, Mommy refused to be shaken. *"Così Fan Tutte,"* she answered. "At the Met. Have you seen it, dear?"

When Mommy disappeared, I was heartbroken but not surprised. I thought she'd gone in search of dresses to wear to the opera and a new car and meat that didn't come from a can. It took months for me to understand that Mommy left not only my father—she also left me.

My mother took me to see every movie that starred a black woman, from *Claudine* to *Foxy Brown*. In the grocery store or any place that was big enough to put a crowd between us, we'd call out the closing lines from *Mahogany*, the movie that Mommy said was the best love story she had seen in a long time, maybe ever. The film stars Billy Dee Williams as a community-minded activist running for Chicago alderman. Diana Ross, an aspiring fashion designer, finds fame and fortune as a model in Italy. Billy Dee, being the righteous brother he is, doesn't dig the shallow Italian fashion scene and splits. At the end of the movie, Diana Ross shows up at one of Billy Dee's Chicago rallies. She hides herself in the crowd and calls out to him. When the two of us recited these lines, Mommy started things off as Diana Ross.

"I'm a widow from the South Side," she'd call out.

"Who said that?" I'd yell back, in the deepest voice I could muster.

"My old man left me with six kids. He ain't been home for weeks and they all got the flu," Mommy said, her smile as bright as Christmas.

"Will the lady who said that please step forward?" I'd yell again, pretending not to see her.

"Mr. Walker, when you're elected, what are you going to do to help me?"

"Well, madam, do you want me to help you with your landlord?"

"Hell no," Mommy answered, a devilish gleam in her eye. "I want you to get me my old man back!"

Mommy swooned over black love stories, reminding me that they were few and far between, but nothing peeled her paint like a butt-kicking adventure flick. No surprise then, when Black Liberation Army leader Assata Shakur broke out of prison, both Mommy and Daddy sat riveted before the screen. My father watched for the politics. Mommy watched for the action.

Convicted of killing a New Jersey state trooper in a highway shootout that left one police officer and one Liberation Army comrade dead, Shakur was sentenced to life in prison, although she was severely wounded in the shootings as well. She served five years of hard time—most of it in solitary confinement, followed by another brutal year spent in a West Virginia federal prison, where her fellow inmates were members of the white supremacist Aryan Sisterhood gang. In 1979, she was transferred to the Clinton Correctional Facility in New Jersey, to a tiny maximum-security wing.

Each night, I crawled into my parents' bed to watch the news as the pieces of Assata's story came together. We snuggled, shoulder to shoulder, under the covers, like the three bears before Goldilocks came. We watched CBS, because Mommy liked Walter Cronkite and my father dug the fact that there were two black correspondents on his show: Hal Walker in Germany and Lee Thornton at the White House. Each night, we impatiently waited for the latest word on Assata while the anchors rambled through what passed for news: a bunch of women protesting in Times Square were screaming, "Two-four-six-eight, pornography is woman hate." Someone threw a lemon coconut cake at the governor of California. He wiped a fingerful of icing off his cheek and proclaimed it delicious. All before we could get to our girl.

That's how my parents described Assata. She was either "our girl" as in "I wonder where our girl is hiding?" Or she was "old girl" as in "Old girl done pissed off a bunch of white folks." Each night we learned a little more of her story and each night she seemed less like a criminal and more like family. Really exciting family. On the second night, the television revealed that Assata had given birth to a baby girl only months before. Less than a week after Assata had given birth, her baby was taken away. Mommy shook her head furiously at the television, as if she could negate the truth of what we saw. "Can't take a baby from a mommy like that," she said, pulling me closer. "I know where she went. She went to get her child and punish the people who took her away."

On the third night, we learned how Assata's escape went down. Using forged driver's licenses and Social Security cards, three men applied for visitation privileges with Assata. On November 2, they met in the visitor's waiting room and managed to make it through registration without being processed by handheld metal detectors, although the sign above their heads said clearly, all visitors were to be searched.

The men—two black, one white—overtook the guards and shuttled Assata to a parked van. Because only the maximum-security portion of the prison was fenced in, they were able to make it to an open field where they met two waiting female comrades. The party split into two vehicles: a blue sedan and a Ford Maverick. They were never seen again.

All those movies I'd watched with Mommy. All those tantalizing tag lines. "They call her Coffy and she'll cream you!" "She had a body men would die for, and a lot of men did!" "A chick with drive who don't take no jive!" Then there was Assata on the television news, a real-life Bonnie with three Clydes to bust her loose. In the theaters, Clint Eastwood was the man because he escaped from Alcatraz. But Assata made even Clint look soft, just a player at her game. It was 1979 and escape was heavy in the air.

Later, when I was much older, I realized that it was no accident that my mother left us in November. She saw Assata on TV and she wasn't thinking, "Beautiful, revolutionary sister," the way my father did or, "Don't mess around with Foxy Brown," the way I did. Mommy saw Assata breaking out and she thought, "Me too." Me too.

Full House

My Father

spent most nights away from home, working. If he didn't have a show, then he was out in the clubs, getting to know people. Some nights, when I complained about being left home alone and hearing strange sounds in the apartment, he'd smuggle me into a disco and deposit me at a booth in the corner with a ginger ale and an order: don't get up, don't walk around, don't move, even to use the bathroom.

When we drove up to a club like Ecstasy or the Soul Kitchen, there was a long line of people waiting in front. From the backseat of my father's car, the line of disco dancers was a gaggle of exotic birds that rustled as they strutted by, a flurry of bright colors, feathers, sequins, gold. We did not wait in line, ever. Daddy eased his car around the back, where an action-hero-sized bouncer ushered us in through a secret passageway. At a country club or a bar mitzvah, coming in through the back door meant we were the help. At the night clubs, coming in the back way meant we were royalty. Daddy was becoming a big shot; he told me so. Our living room wall was lined with photographs of him and all the famous people he met: Evelyn "Champagne" King, Ashford and Simpson, Stephanie Mills, Stevie Wonder.

I'd help Daddy set up his equipment backstage, then take my place in the appointed booth. At Ecstasy, the DJ booth was up high in what looked like a solid-gold egg, floating in the sky. The DJ wobbled his neck back and forth like a chicken, while on the turntables, he spun rhythm and beats. My father taught me everything I knew about music, from Nat King Cole to Curtis Mayfield to Marlena Shaw and Teena Marie. But he said the discos were more than a good place to shake your groove thing, he said that discos were an example of our changing world. The only white folks you ever saw in our neighborhood were the mailman, the police, and the shopkeepers, but there were all kinds of people at the nightclubs. White guys in preppy oxford shirts and V-neck sweaters, Asian girls with Dorothy Hamill haircuts, beautiful Puerto Rican guys, looking like Freddie Prinze in their white muscle shirts. I'd watch the people dancing and never get bored.

I'd met Daddy's friends a few times at the house, but I didn't really get to know them until after Mommy left. Uncle Roger reminded me of Isaac Hayes. He was *Ebony Man* handsome with a smooth cue-ball head and a thick, scraggly beard. He owned a moving company and had the muscle to prove it. Daddy's other friend, Sammy, was a goofball, always late and cracking jokes. Reed thin and daffodil yellow, Sammy worked part time for Uncle Roger. But really, he didn't seem to have any bigger aspiration in life than to follow Daddy and Uncle Roger around. As Daddy said, when he mimicked Sammy's screechy falsetto, "You know, Teddo. I just want to be down."

Sometimes, one of Daddy's buddies would ask me to dance and lead me out onto the dance floor. For four or five incredible minutes, I was out there, doing my thing, pretending I was Diana Ross or Donna Summer, shaking my little hips as I turned, singing along with the crowd.

Eleven o'clock on Thursday, a school night, and I was with Daddy at the Soul Kitchen. The DJ announced that Daddy was about to begin his show. Barry White's Love Unlimited Orchestra played softly in the background and Daddy did a slow hustle out onto the stage. Daddy never rushed his entrance. He took his time. He had arrived that night dressed in a green polyester suit, a safari-print silk shirt unbuttoned to his chest, a gold medallion with his Zodiac sign, Cancer, hanging from his neck. But for the show, he had changed into a creaseless black tuxedo. Then he grabbed the mike from the MC like he was Al Green about to testify on the subject of his broken heart and he growled, "Good evening." In a voice that sizzled like hot butter in a pan, Daddy said, "My name is Teddo, the Amazing Magician. But you can call me . . . the Magic Man."

From the bar, a woman in a feather headdress called out, "Well, all right now."

The lady sitting next to her tossed a headful of Sister Sledge curls and purred, "Go on with your bad self, honey."

Daddy walked up to the biggest, baddest brother in the club and said, "I know a lot of you don't believe in magic." He reached behind the brother's ear and grabbed a quarter. "I know that you think tricks are for kids," reaching into the other ear, he pulled out a bright yellow scarf, attached to a twenty-dollar bill.

"I'm not here to convince you that I can do magic. I'm here to issue a warning." He picked up a newspaper from the bar and asked the bartender for a glass of water. He folded the paper in half, then folded it again and poured the water into the paper. Then he dramatically opened every page asking, "What happened to the water?"

He folded the paper up and asked the bartender for a fresh glass. Then he tilted the paper sideways and poured a full glass of water. "I said I had a warning," Daddy said with a sly grin. "And the warning is this: you can't believe what you read in the papers. They say what goes up must come down. They say there's no such thing as magic. Hell, they said we'd never send a man to the moon. I've been to the moon. I was the first man on the moon! But you know they couldn't let it be known that a black man beat the white man in the space race! So they keep it on the hush-hush."

"Sho, you're right," called out a heavyset man from the first row. His skin was berry brown and his face bobbled, a sweaty round balloon above a black shirt and a red suit.

Then the Magic Man turned around, tapped his cane on the side of the bar, and asked the crowd to examine it from every angle. He walked out onto the dance floor, threw the cane into the air, and a dove appeared. While Sammy chased the bird, Daddy faced the audience with a huge grin. He took off his jacket and rolled up his sleeves with a flourish.

"Nothing up my sleeves, but arms. I won't tell you it's magic, but aren't you beginning to wonder if you should get your eyes checked?"

There were giggles all around, and the man in the red suit let out a walloping belly laugh.

"Now ladies and gentlemen, I'd like you to all participate in an experiment with me," Daddy said. "The scientific name is transference, but you might know it as mind reading."

Daddy walked toward the DJ booth and, lifting his arms, said, "Maestro, a little mood music."

The hypnotic notes of Dizzy Gillespie's "Moon in Tunisia" began to float above the room.

"Tonight, I'm going to prove to you that anyone can be a mind reader. Everyone in this room will be a part of this trick, so you might want to put the liquor down and pay attention. First, we're going to need a volunteer."

A few women put their hands up in the air.

"Let's not make this so easy," he said. "Last time, I chose a lovely lady. Don't any of you brothers want to show us the power of your intellect?"

A few guys raised their hands. Daddy chose a blond guy in a black turtleneck and a charcoal gray suit.

"Thank you, sir," Daddy said, reaching out to shake his hand. "Your name is . . ."

"Billy," the man said.

"Billy what?" Daddy asked.

"Billy Davidson," the man answered.

"Everyone give a round of applause for my good friend, Billy Dee!" Daddy said, and the room whooped it up.

Daddy took out a deck of cards and fanned it front of the man. "Select a card, and take it out carefully so I can't see it. Look at it, memorize the card, and put it in your pocket."

"I want you to focus all of your energy on that card," Daddy said, walking around the man and shooting invisible bolts of energy at him through his fingertips. "Does anyone in the audience get a mental image of Billy Dee's card? Please raise your hand."

No one in the room raised a hand.

Daddy looked worried. "Billy Dee, are you focusing on the card? You're not thinking about your girlfriend or what you're going to have for breakfast in the morning, are you? 'Cause you're part of my act now and I need your full attention."

"You've got it, man," Billy Dee said, smiling.

Daddy smiled back. "Let me give you a little help. What you need is a thinking cap."

Daddy reached behind his little stand and pulled out a big gold turban. It was adorned with a fake ruby in the front and a gigantic white feather. Everyone laughed just at the sight of it. Daddy helped Billy Dee put the turban on.

"Okay, I want you to think of the card again. Focus all of your energy on that card. If anyone in the audience begins to experience transference and can also see the card, please raise your hand."

Immediately, twenty hands went up. We could all see the jack of spades rising out of the turban.

"I believe that this old thinking cap is doing the trick. What do you see, young lady?"

"Jack of spades."

"How about you, sir?" Daddy called on another person in the audience.

"Jack of spades."

"Since three's a charm, will the woman in the back, the one wearing the roller skates, tell me what card she is *sensing* is Billy Dee's card?"

"Jack of spades."

"Billy Dee, what is your card? May I see it?"

The man held up his card, the jack of spades.

"Thank you very much, young man," Daddy said. "You've helped me demonstrate that all of our elementary-school teachers were right. You can accomplish anything if you put on your thinking cap."

The crowd responded with laughter and applause. I was afraid of Daddy getting heckled, especially in nightclubs where people came to dance, not see a magic show. But it almost never happened. People loved Daddy. They just wanted entertainment. The disco was a grown-up Romper Room and all the dancers were really just big kids.

Daddy walked over to a woman holding a large handbag and said, "You're clutching that bag so tight. Must be afraid of pickpockets."

"Can't be too careful," she muttered.

Daddy asked her to repeat the words into the microphone. "Make sure everybody hears you."

"Can't be too careful," she said louder, then she sucked her teeth and straightened her blond Afro wig.

"Do you mind if I look into your bag?" Daddy asked. The woman rolled her eyes, but handed the bag over anyway.

Daddy examined the contents with a flourish. "Wallet. Lipstick. Cigarettes. You know you shouldn't smoke."

He handed the bag back to the woman. Then he turned to the audience and asked, "What if I told you that this woman has stolen something from me? Shouldn't I give her bag another look? After all, what did she say?"

Then the entire room repeated, "Can't be too careful."

Daddy asked the woman to please bring him her handbag. She strutted over to him. "I know you're not accusing me of stealing something from you, Magic Man."

He laughed and walked to the center of the dance floor, tugged open the handles of the bag, and pulled our rabbit out. "I'm going to need my bunny back, darling."

♣

The DJ began playing Daddy's exit music. Barry White was asking if I was a real woman because he was, most certainly, a real man. Daddy thanked the audience and strolled, in three-quarter time, off the dance floor and disappeared backstage. The applause was hearty and I joined in, clapping until my hands were sore. I knew that Daddy listened carefully to the level of applause and a tepid finish to his show would ruin his evening.

"I've seen those tricks a hundred times," Uncle Roger said. "Brother's got something. Charisma or something." I just nodded and smiled.

A woman in an orange kimono top and matching pants came over to our table. Her skin was dark brown and her hair was jet black, cut in a razor-sharp bob. She was pretty, like Beverly Johnson on the cover of *Essence* magazine. I kept staring at her. One side was curled under and fell over her eye, the other side was pulled up with a beaded comb. It was a style my mother would've liked.

Mommy loved her hair—she worked hard to keep it long and straight. My father kept telling her to get an Afro like Angela Davis, his dream woman. He told everyone I was named after her, though I was already two when my father bought his first "Free Angela Davis" T-shirt. My birth certificate read Angela Esther Brown, Angela being the name of my maternal grandmother, Esther being the name of my paternal grandmother. But from the minute my father began calling me Angela Davis Brown, even Mommy thought it was a righteous idea. It didn't hurt that adding Davis to my name was a handy way of evicting my paternal grandmother from her namesake. I never knew my grandma

Esther but Mommy told me she was "one half Native American, one quarter white, and all evil." She thought Mommy was way too dark to marry my red-boned father, and she let it be known at every turn. Not exactly the way to break up a courtship in 1965, black being so beautiful and my father anxious to make up for his ancestors' past sins.

The way my parents talked about hair was as predictable as the dialogue of a movie that I watched over and over again. My father said that Mommy's straightened hair showed a plantation mentality. Mommy held out her arm. "Look, Teddo, I'm black as night. I won't ever, can't ever, forget what that means. I don't need an Afro pick with a black fist on the top to remind me I live in America." Ignoring her, my father said that if her politics were in the right place, she would walk the walk and stop pressing her hair. Mommy called him a "high yella nigga, with too much to prove." My father could never top that.

Once a month, Mommy got her hair straightened at a salon called Ebony Styles. She kept that money separate, hidden, so my father did not find it. We had to be truly broke for her to dip into her straightening money. When there was no money and she could not get her hair done professionally, she took out my grandmother's old pressing comb and rested it on the stove. The comb was black and heavy, crisp, like a pan that won't ever come clean. We'd sit in the kitchen and watch the comb in the flames, as the kitchen filled with the smell of burning hair. I did not like the smell, but Mommy said I wasn't smelling deep enough.

"You've got to learn to conjure the spirits in a thing," she told me. It was a Saturday and she wore an African print caftan that my father bought for her. The dress was gold and navy blue, with hints of red and white. She looked beautiful in it, mahogany and patrician. Like Cicely Tyson on the cover of a Miles Davis album. Her hair hung straight and curled, slightly, around her shoulders. She stood behind me like an African priestess and I shivered slightly. "Close your eyes," she said. "Smell the hot comb. Go back in time, fifty years. Your Nana, my grandmother's mother, is living in Harlem. She buys this hot comb after saving for three months. She works in the Pepsi bottle factory in Queens and that's a whole week's worth of wages. She straightens her hair to go out that Saturday night."

I turned to look at her and laugh, but she spun me around and told me to keep my eyes closed. "From my Nana to my mother to me. A thousand afternoons spent in kitchens just like this, around tables just like this. Dressing for nights out dancing and nights of mourning. Funerals and weddings and christenings. This is a woman's space. If the teeth in that comb could talk, they would tell a history of black women. Your father doesn't understand. It has nothing to do with white women at all. It's got nothing to do with wanting to look like white women. I can't say it didn't start out that way, but it sure doesn't end that way. That comb is mine and it will be yours, regardless of what you want to do with your hair." At the time, I wore my hair in long braids, adorned with beads, a hairstyle that both my parents approved.

She knelt in front of me then. "Angela, do you know what an heirloom is?" she asked.

I shook my head no.

"It's something valuable that belongs to a family, that's passed from generation to generation," she said. "It could be a piece of jewelry or a work of art."

"Like a painting?"

"Exactly."

She told me we didn't have anything like that. All we had was the comb. So when she put it on the fire and I smelled that burning smell, she told me, I shouldn't listen to my father. The scent of hair straightening was not the smell of the oppressor. I should listen to my mother. Dig deeper into that smell. Smell the women of our family, sitting around a kitchen table. Smell their history and their journeys. Smell them sweating their curls out on the dance floors of Harlem nightclubs. Smell their tears as they followed the procession of the night funerals the old folks used to have. Smell them wanting to be beautiful for their men. Smell their desire. Smell their longing. Smell them wanting. Know they loved me and they had nothing more to give me than an old pressing comb. No, this was not a cameo pin, with the silhouette of a fancy lady, or luxurious gold earrings that sat heavy in your hand. But the comb possessed its own value. Mommy said that sometimes, when she was feeling absolutely exhausted, she took out the comb and just held it. She felt the comb's weight and was reminded of her Nana's and her mother's strength. She said to remember the meaning of the word "jewel." It wasn't just something that could be worn, like a diamond, on your finger or around your neck. She hugged me then and without another word, turned around and began to press her hair.

I did not need to smell the hot comb burning to know that Mommy left it in my drawer to keep me strong while she was gone. I was convinced that she left me a note, perhaps many notes, to tell me she loved me, why she was going, and when she was coming back. But my father must have thrown them away, destroyed or hidden them. He was the magician, and surely he made Mommy disappear. Leaving around correspondence from my mother was tantamount to throwing the audience a manual to his tricks. He preferred, demanded, that Mommy's disappearance be shrouded in mystery, cloaked by illusion. He was all the family I had then and he ran the show. My father required not only my applause, but my faith and devotion. In time, I developed my own act—magician's assistant, spectator in awe, adoring daughter.

It took me a long time to stop jumping every time the phone rang. My father eyed my skittish gestures but did not question me. By the time we'd lived a month without her, it became clear that Mommy was not going to call. He knew that; it must have been in the note.

When he went out for meetings or to perform, I searched his room carefully. Aware that my father's messes composed their own unreadable order, I did not search greedily. I looked at one drawer, one box, one suitcase at a time. I looked for my Aunt Mona's number in his address book but found nothing. Boldly, I called information in Chicago, knowing that the long-distance calls were itemized on the bill. But Aunt Mona wasn't listed and my father never mentioned the charge. Bold, again, I dialed another 312 number and tried my grandma Esther's number, even though I knew she was dead. The woman who answered the phone wasn't my Aunt Mona. She didn't even speak English. Within weeks, I settled into the nest of my father's misdirection. But when my father announced we were moving, I knew better than to fight him. I also knew what to do.

The next day, I left a little early for school. I walked down the dingy hallway of our building, past 5B where Dwayne Irving lived. He was a high school boy I had a crush on. The girls in the building said he looked like an orangutan because his arms hung so far past his knees. But I thought he was beautiful, graceful with a slow and bounding stride. If I was another type of girl, I would have talked to Dwayne Irving as he loped by. I would have told him about Mommy, begged him to look out for her, kissed him before we moved, and vowed to keep in touch. But I wasn't that girl. I walked past 5F where Melba Bailey lived. For five minutes, the year before, she was my best friend. It turned out that she was only having a fight with Gerina Richie, her real best friend, and used me to make Gerina jealous. She'd dropped me so fast, I'd nearly gotten rug burns. The day she and Gerina made up, she pretended not to see me in the playground, before school.

"Do you hear someone talking?" she'd asked Gerina with a snicker.

"No, I think it's just the wind," Gerina said, grinning right at me.

Then they'd linked arms and walked away together. Melba hadn't spoken to me since.

I pressed the black elevator button and stared at the chocolate brown door. The elevators were painted just last summer, but Mommy found the color no improvement on the chipping gray. "Shit brown," she declared, each and every time she saw it. The brown door slid open and I rode six floors to the basement by myself. I did not ring the bell of Mr. Hernandez, our super. I wasn't prepared to explain my story or read his face for some feature, some expression I could trust. I simply slipped the letter underneath his door. On the envelope, I wrote: "Please hold for my mother, Melanie Brown. Please do not give this to my father. —Angela D. Brown."

♣

I was eleven, that winter when Mommy disappeared. My father and I moved into the top floor of a Brooklyn brownstone. This was our fifth apartment in two years. We moved whenever Daddy got a "great deal" on a "fabulous place." I gave up on making friends. Daddy said I was asocial, like Mommy. He said if I was going to get anywhere in life, then I needed to be more of a people person. I told him that I was a people person—a mother and a father type of person. That ended that conversation.

Our new apartment was a long, shotgun-style tunnel of inter-connecting rooms. There were two front doors and a small bathroom off the kitchen. Even in the daytime, the rooms were dark, musty like a cave. But the living room featured big parlor windows that let in butter sun. When I pushed aside all of Daddy's magic stuff, there was so much room I could roller-skate. We didn't have much furniture. In the late afternoon, when the sun cast shadows across the bare walls, I'd dress up in my pink satin short shorts, the ones with the white piping all around, and pretend that I was at the roller rink and that the shadows were disco lights. The stereo was in my room, and sometimes, I'd play one of Daddy's newer albums. Donna Summer was my favorite, and I'd dance and skate across the living room. I sang as I spun in circles around the room. I first heard the song after Mommy left and I secretly believed that the words were written about me, or someone just like me. Who else could she mean when she sang, "Bad girls, sad girls, you such a dirty bad girl. Beep-beep. Uh-uh." Every other kid at my school had a father who'd skipped out on them, but everybody had a mother. Everybody.

In the days after Mommy's disappearance, my hair did its own mourning. My braids, once as thick and shiny as a brand-new bag of licorice, grew dull and fuzzy. I did not know how to re-create the intertwined strands of hair that fell from my scalp like vines, and I missed Mommy, the green thumb who made everything in my garden grow. After two weeks, even my father noticed how dirty and matted my hair was becoming. I was still loath to touch it. Mommy had braided my hair, maybe for the last time. But when the kids at school took their behind-my-back comments to my face and the teacher sent a note home declaring serious concern for my personal hygiene, I gave in.

My father said that we were not to tell anyone about Mommy's disappearance. He warned me that "the state" did not look fondly upon his line of work and the unsteady income. I later found out that my father had not filed taxes for years. Almost all of his clients paid him in cash. But I did not need to know about the state of my father's income taxes to understand the severity of his warning when he said that without my mother, I could be taken away from him and put in a foster home.

"We have to keep up a good front, okay, princess?" he said, standing behind me one evening as I brushed my teeth in the tiny bathroom with only a shower, no tub. He peered at me in the mirror and I spit out my mouthful of toothpaste. "Clean as a whip, okay? And comb that hair."

I went into my room and closed the door and from underneath my mattress, I pulled out my treasures. Mommy's hot comb. My parents' wedding picture. I sat my treasures in my lap and then I started. It took me all night to undo those braids. Each unraveled strand was a loss, a little square of blackboard where Mommy's words were being erased. One braid might have spelled out "mother." Another might have spelled out "daughter." A third might have spelled "dream." More braids, more words. Touch. Heart. Jump. Fly. Eat. Sleep. Read. Kiss. Bury. Plant. Grow. And in the back of my head, the braid that was so long it tickled the hollow between my shoulders. Loyalty. I dispatched memories and hopes like that, all night long, each braid unraveled and another word erased, until my hair was one wild mass of naps, too long to be an Afro, too unruly for words. A head full of hair sticking out in every direction like antennae, trying to pick up a New York station. Mommy, are you listening?

As long as I could remember, I grumbled about having my hair done. Mommy sat at the edge of her bed, an arsenal of weapons laid out across the blue-green bedspread: a comb with wide teeth for plowing the kinky parts; a comb with fine teeth for unraveling the tip of a braid and for combing out my baby hair when the style was done; a jar of grease—TCB or Soft Sheen, depending on what was on sale; a pink plastic spray bottle with a mixture of water and setting lotion; a Ziploc bag of bubbles, clips, and rainbow-colored rubberbands.

I'd sit on the floor, on a pillow between Mommy's legs. During the summer, I'd rest my head on the inside of her thigh which somehow, miraculously, was cool. When the weather was cold, I'd press my cheek to her thigh and feel warmth. Once she was gone, I remembered those feelings—cool in the summertime, warm in the winter—and I tried to figure out how it could have been I felt all of those things and whether or not this was just another thing I'd romanticized or plain old remembered wrong. And I think it had less to do with the actual temperature of Mommy's skin and more to do with the way it made me feel, which was just right.

Mommy said that I was tender-headed because I yelped when she combed out my hair. After she left and I combed my own hair, I learned that the comb feels different when it's in your own hand. I could spend hours, sprawled out on my father's bed, on his ocean blue bedspread, combing my hair until the strands turned soft and wooly. Mommy left and I wasn't tender-headed anymore, just tenderhearted.

My father offered to take me to the hair salon to get my hair braided, but I refused. I didn't want Mommy to come home and find me with some other woman's braids all flounced around my head. Not to mention, I was just a little suspicious about what someone could do with a lock of my hair. Mommy always flushed the hair left on the comb when she was done styling it. She said that *her* mother told her that if the birds made a nest with a lock of your hair, you'd go crazy. When I asked her why, she seemed surprised at the question, as if the logic was plain enough to see. "It's the *pecking* that makes you crazy," she said, tapping at my temple like a typewriter key.

I did not learn how to braid my hair, not being able to see the back of my head the way I needed to. But I washed my hair weekly, then I combed it out and put it in a ponytail. Or I'd part my hair in two and wear it in little Afro-puffs. Simple stuff. Sometimes, when Mommy combed my hair, she used to do a zigzag part. After she greased it, that part shone like a lightning bolt. On those days—first day of school, big test day—she'd kiss my scalp when she was done and say, "You are electric, baby!" And all day, I'd walk around feeling crazy confident like a superhero, like I was Storm from the X-Men and I could make it thunder with a blink of my eyes.

A month after Mommy was gone, there was still no word. No divorce papers, no custody arrangements, no indication at all that I was more than the toothbrush she left behind. Pink with splayed bristles, I kept it anyway and added it to my treasures.

My father had no answers. No, he didn't know where she was. Yes, everything was going to be okay. I asked Daddy to sit on the bed and then I sat on a pillow on the floor between his legs.

"Pretend to comb my hair."

"Angela, honey, you know I don't know how to do your hair."

I began to cry then. "It doesn't matter, Daddy. Just pretend."

I sat in the hollow of his legs and pressed my face against his pant leg, which was neither cool nor warm, but I grabbed his leg anyway until the tears came freely and my father's pants were soaked.

"Oh, Angela," he said. "Oh, Angela, baby, please."

I think it scared him. Me, a growing girl, sitting between his legs. Daddy was funny about things like that. Even when I was little, he didn't like me crawling into his lap. He said, "You have to be careful the way you behave with girl children." I know it made him sad the way I sobbed. So whenever I asked him to let me sit between his legs for him to pretend to comb my hair, he said, "Sure, sugar. Sure."

Miss Black America

A new wave

of missing Mommy hit me with the first string of holiday lights I saw in our neighbor's front window. Christmas hurt so bad. The caroling and the gaudy decorations. I'd been too hopeless to give my father the usual elaborate wish list that I'd given Mommy, afraid that he'd get mad or moody or, worse, declare Christmas canceled. I had no doubt he could play high Grinch, if motivated. Secretly, I hoped to come home from school and find out that he'd been the busiest elf in all of Brooklyn: putting together our tree, wrapping presents, even putting up a few decorations in the window.

What I missed the most that December was the food. Mommy never baked cakes or pies, though she did a very good job of keeping the pantry stocked with my favorite Keebler's chocolate chip cookies. But Mommy could cook. On special occasions, she broke out exotic dishes from the treasure trove that my father referred to, with wicked glee, as the "boyfriend recipes."

There were the Puerto Rican dishes she'd learned from her high school boyfriend's mother. This woman, Señora Elsa, taught Mommy she should learn to cook something special from a man's homeland. Señora Elsa taught Mommy that a familiar dish, expertly rendered, could smooth out any rough spot in the relationship. Mommy took her advice to heart. Sometimes, Mommy made jerk chicken and a vegetable rundown: carrots, sweet potatoes, and cabbage cooked in coconut milk until the juices ran down the side of the pot. Other times, she made a Haitian dish called djon djon, confetti-colored rice with bits of scallion, bacon, green and red pepper. When I was sick, she made an African peanut soup out of nothing but chicken, a can of tomatoes, an onion, and a half jar of Jif peanut butter.

I begged her to tell me the names of the boyfriends who inspired these meals, but she claimed to have forgotten them. When I pressed her to try harder, she said, "Why do I need to remember their names when I can taste them in the food?"

When Mommy was falling in love with my father, she made him fried porgies. This was neither a dish he'd ever loved nor was it a specialty of Pittsburgh, where my father grew up. But Mommy said that when she'd pressed my father for a favorite dish and he couldn't really name one, she vowed to make him a meal he would never forget. After searching for weeks, she decided that there was a kind of matrimonial poetry to the combination of cornmeal, crab boil, and sizzling fish. She called the dish Melanie's I Loves You Porgy and she made it every Sunday. My father ate the fish so drenched with Tabasco Sauce it was redder than a snapper. What I truly loved was knowing that she did not make Daddy's special dish if she was angry at him. She never battered her frustration in cornmeal. When Mommy was really, really mad, she didn't cook at all.

I did not think then that Mommy had left me as much as I thought she had left my father. And left me with him. There was so much about my father Mommy couldn't stand. She was not charmed by his magic tricks. She did not like the nightclubs where he performed. She hated the nights when money was so tight dinner consisted of little more than what she called air pudding and nothin' pie. She hated meat that came out of cans, and the only thing she hated more was when there was no meat at all, just rice and beans. She hated that my father's Mercedes was nearly twenty years old. My father called it a classic. Mommy said the car was a pompous money drain.

"I'd rather drive a new Honda than an ancient Mercedes. One day that engine will be beyond repair and we'll be holding the frame up and hoofin' it." She lifted her skirt and made a running in place motion like Fred Flintstone driving his car through Bedrock.

♥

The closer it got to Christmas, the more Mommy's absence felt like punishment. I was hungry for homemade dishes, cooked in our own pots. McDonald's and White Castle were our staples since Mommy ran away from home, but they no longer seemed like much of a treat. The very thought of unwrapping Christmas dinner from a foil wrapper made me feel even sorrier for myself. I began to entertain the idea of cooking Christmas dinner myself.

But Mommy did not write any of the recipes down, not anywhere I could find them. The scraps of paper that I found after my mother left were all useless, all marked with her big round letters. There was a grocery list, magazine subscription cards she never mailed, a to-do list: wash whites, iron Teddo's shirts, mail electric bill on Friday, buy stamps at post office. On the back of bill envelopes, I found doodles with different variations of her name: *Melanie Brown. Melanie Aisha Brown. Melanie A. Brown.* One piece of paper was written with a large *B* in the middle and a small *a* and *m* on either side.

The strangest ones were the autographs with last names that did not match our own. My mother had been born Melanie Lewis. But on these sheets she had written: *Melanie Lark. Melanie Golden. Melanie Davis.*

♥

I was in the grocery store with my father when I got the idea to act out the love scene from *Mahogany* with him.

"I'm a widow from the South Side," I called out from one end of the breakfast cereal aisle.

"Who said that?" my father hollered back.

"My old man left me with six kids. He ain't been home for weeks and they all got the flu," I said, my smile as bright as Christmas.

"Will the lady who said that please step forward?" my father said, moving toward me.

"Mr. Walker when you're elected, what are you going to do to help me?"

"Well, madam, do you want me to help you with your landlord?"

"Hell no," I answered, "I want you to get me my mother back!"

My father turned around, pushed our cart away, and for the next half hour pretended that he had never laid eyes on me in his life.

♥

On the last day of school before the holiday break I came home to find my father doing everything right. He threw out the four-foot plastic tree we owned for years and bought a real one. It smelled of pine and was taller than he was. After covering my father's face with kisses, I went to the closet to pull out our decorations. He stood behind me and pulled me by the waist away from the open closet door.

"I threw them out, okay, darling?" he said. "No decorations this year, just lights."

I nodded, happy to make any concession.

We ate White Castle for dinner that night, but I did not mind at all. We ate our burgers on the floor and spent the evening untangling the strings of lights that my father fished out. We listened to Johnny Mathis singing "White Christmas" and we tested the lights for defective bulbs, pulling them in and out of their tiny sockets, watching them flash on and off.

♥

Christmas morning, the tears hit me, sneaky and powerful like a sunrise. I cried under a tent of bedclothes, which needed washing, until I heard my father stirring in the kitchen. I reached for the door handle, but it didn't give.

I called out for him. "Daddy!"

"I'm not ready for you yet, princess."

I was sure he would skip it, the Christmas morning ritual he'd been doing since he was a little boy. But something sweet was baking in the oven and Curtis Mayfield was on the turntable singing "Keep On Pushing." I sat on the bed, cross-legged in my Spider-Man footy pajamas that Mommy bought for me in the boys' department after I told her to never, ever buy me Barbie clothes again. "Especially not the white one," my father chimed in, backing me up when, the winter before, Mommy bought me a pink-flannel nightgown with a gigantic blond Barbie face emblazoned across the front.

I heard the door give and saw my father balancing a TV tray with all the grace of a waiter in a fancy French restaurant.

"Mademoiselle," he said. "Breakfast is served." Breakfast was a hot cup of strawberry Quik for me, coffee for Daddy, and two Hostess cupcakes.

I held the confection in my hand. "This is Jesus' birthday cake?"

"Come on, Angela," he said. "Don't be such a brat. I warmed it up in the oven and everything."

♥

When my father was little, my grandma Esther didn't let him get out of bed until breakfast was brought to him. "Little John P. Ghetto," Mommy said when she thought my father was acting spoiled. "Just because your mother treated you like a prince, doesn't mean I have to."

My grandmother made a coffee cake with icing and called it Jesus' birthday cake. Despite her grumbling, Mommy loved the tradition and continued it after my grandmother passed. I figured that this year, Jesus' birthday cake was the last thing on my father's mind. I was wrong.

"You say grace," my father said, holding both of my hands in his. Christmas was the only day of the year that I ever saw my father pray.

"Thank you God, for another Christmas," I said. "And happy birthday to your son Jesus. Please bless my father. Please bless me. Please bless Mommy wherever she is."

My father jerked his hands away from mine. His face was a circle of dirty weather.

"Why'd you have to mention her?" he asked. "This is *our* Christmas, Angela!"

Anxious to fix things, I asked my father if I could open up my Christmas presents and he seemed to recover. I followed him into the living room and we both sat, cross-legged, in front of the tree.

"Why don't you open the presents from your mother first?" His voice was pure venom.

I pretended not to hear him and reached for the gift closest to me. He grabbed my hand so hard that the skin vibrated like the top of a trampoline.

"There are *no* presents from your mother because she's a selfish bitch."

"Okay, Daddy," I whispered, too frightened to shed the fresh tears that pressed against the back of my eyes.

"No," he said, rising to stand above me. "Don't you 'Okay, Daddy' me. I want you to repeat after me, 'There are no presents from my mother because she is a selfish bitch.'"

I coughed then as if I'd swallowed something and it went down the wrong way. I pounded my chest dramatically and mimed that he should get me a glass of water, but Daddy was not feeling merciful. He handed me his cup of coffee and it tasted like a cold dirt milkshake.

Once my coughs subsided, he repeated, "There are no presents—"

I cut him off and then said the thing he'd ordered me to say. He was silent then and stared at me as if I was a person he'd only met once before, and that being under terrifying circumstances.

"Can I have my presents now?" I said. I was desperate to save Christmas, but afraid to touch the three shiny silver boxes, expertly wrapped with red and green bows. My father's hands were magic, but he was too impatient, too sloppy about those kinds of details, to have ever wrapped those gifts. He must have had them wrapped at the store.

"Do you have any idea where your mother is?" my father asked, ambling over to the glass étagère where my parents kept their records. He took off Curtis and put on an old Minnie Riperton, one of Mommy's favorites.

I didn't answer.

"Ask me where your mother is, Angela."

I asked him that question, whenever I dared to, in the weeks after Mommy disappeared. "I wish I knew, baby," he said on those occasions. "God only knows, Angela. God only knows."

Now my father was telling me that I should ask him again and I started to shake because I knew that this time, when I asked, he was going to give me an answer that might break me past the point of fixing. My mouth fell open and, as spit gathered, I sat silent.

"Let me put it a different way," my father said, in full performance mode. "Did it ever occur to you that your mother might be dead, Angela?"

♥

I was eleven years old the first Christmas I contemplated suicide. I did not know anything about the culture of suicides. I did not know that the right combination of pills could do the trick or that sometimes, people sliced their wrists. What I knew was that in school, we were taught of the Great Depression and how when some people lost all of their money, they jumped out of windows. That was the idea—1920s stockbrokers, and Mommy meaning more than money—that propelled me from the floor near the Christmas tree to the living room window. I was quick and I did not worry about wings. But the paint around the windowsill was thick. The window did not open. I crawled onto the ledge and pressed my hands and cheek against the cold glass. Could I break through the glass? How much would that hurt? My father grabbed me by the collar of my Spider-Man pajamas and threw me on the floor.

"What the hell are you doing?" he asked, and the tone in his voice was half scared, half annoyed that I'd interrupted his performance in such scene-stealing fashion.

"You said she was dead!" I hollered, my face wet with snot and spit, misery and fury.

"No," he answered, philosophically. "I said, did you ever *imagine* that she might be dead?"

I wiped my face with the bottom half of my shirt, then I asked him, "So Mommy isn't dead?"

"Of course not," he said, putting his arms around me as if he only now understood what I was willing to do at the prospect of such news. "She's living in California. Hollywood. Can you fucking believe that?"

♥

I knew then why my mother had left without taking me with her. Why there was no note. Why she was not coming back. A month before she disappeared my mother had taken me to a competition. She said it was an "open call." It was for a pageant, Miss Black New York City. The way she had dressed up, I thought we were going shopping. Somewhere fancy. On Madison Avenue, maybe. But instead of getting off the train in Midtown, we rode all the way into Brooklyn. We walked down Flatbush Avenue, to a gigantic old theater, and there were maybe a hundred women standing outside. They were all dressed in high heels and stockings. They were all in full makeup. And this is when I knew the "open call" was serious business: at least half of the women were as pretty as Mommy. We joined the end of the line and Mommy whispered in my ear, "If anyone asks, you are my niece, not my daughter. Don't call me Mommy, call me Melanie. And I am twenty-four years old. Don't look surprised when you hear me say it."

It took us nearly two hours just to get inside and get an application. As my mother filled out the papers, I read the flyer carefully. "Miss Black New York City is a not-for-profit organization and an official preliminary to the Miss Black New York and Miss Black America pageants. We provide scholarships to our winner as well as affording her an opportunity to be a visible presence in our city at both speaking and entertainment events. We truly believe that competing in Miss Black New York City is an experience that furthers young women personally and professionally, building character, poise, confidence, and all the qualities essential for success in today's modern world."

Mommy finished her application and took it to the front of the theater where the pageant officials sat like the three wise men, except they were women. They were all grandmother age and each of them was dressed in Afrocentric robes or dresses. One woman wore her hair in braids. The other wore a short Afro. The third woman wore an African-print hat that looked like a crown. It was the woman with the crown who took the sheet from Mommy.

"Everything appears to be in order," she said, without looking up. "Melanie Aisha Brown. Birthdate: October 8, 1955. May I see your driver's license, Melanie?"

My mother grabbed her purse as if the woman might take it away from her to check for the license herself. "I d-d-d-on't have a driver's license."

The woman nodded. "No problem. Come back tomorrow with your birth certificate."

"My birth certificate was lost."

"Passport?"

"I've never been abroad."

"I understand." The woman turned to look at me. "Do you go everywhere with your mother?"

I smiled and nodded yes.

"Silly girl," my mother said, pulling me close to her. "This isn't my daughter. This is my niece. Am I your favorite auntie, Angela?"

I nodded yes.

"Do you wish sometimes that I was your mother, Angela?"

I nodded yes again.

The woman did not address Mommy at all. "How old are you, Angela?"

"Eleven."

"Well, in six years come back and see us. You could be Miss Black New York City." Then she turned to Mommy and handed her the application. "Take good care of that little girl, Mrs. Brown."

"Mrs.?" my mother asked. "I'm not married! This isn't my little girl!" Her voice was high and flustered.

The woman looked beyond Mommy and waved the next contestant to the desk.

Mommy held my hand tight as we walked down the long aisle of the theater. The seats were old and some of the stuffing burst through the red chair cushions, but it was still a beautiful place. The chandeliers were bigger than I'd ever seen and I wondered if this was what it was like at the Metropolitan Opera.

Outside, Mommy was silent and I followed her around the corner wondering what I could say to make up for my mistake. She stopped near the back door of the theater. I started to speak and she put up both hands and said, "Don't." She pulled two tokens from her coat pocket and handed one to me. It was her good coat, nubby brown with a black rabbit fur collar. She was wearing thigh-high boots and a purple wraparound dress. She had saved for weeks to buy a matching purple hat and purple gloves. She had pulled on one glove and seemed to be readying to pull on a second when she took her bare hand and slapped me. The first slap brought tears. On the second slap, I dropped my token on the sidewalk. The third slap was pure pain. By the fifth slap, I was just praying for it to stop. She slapped me eleven times. She did not count aloud, but each slap was so measured, so controlled, that I was able to keep track. She hit me, pulled her hand back, paused, looked at her hand, looked at me, then slapped me again. Over and over, eleven times. Like the birthday punches boys gave each other at school. Then she put a purple glove on the hand that had been bare and I followed her to the subway. She threw the pageant application away before we boarded the train. When we got home, I did not need her to tell me that everything about the day was a secret to be kept from my father. A month later, she was gone.

♥

"Your mother thinks she's going to be a movie star," my father said, still holding me close. "Can you believe that?" He said this as if he was a man who did not earn his living pulling rabbits out of hats. It was like hearing Pinocchio talk about Alice, and how she needed to grow up and stop fooling around in Wonderland.

"She always thought she was too good for us," my father said. "Miss Dark and Lovely. But that's okay. We don't need her. She'll be back and when she comes, we won't care."

He got up and began to pace the living room. Although my father was never a smoker, he had a smoker's worried, pensive way of walking floors.

"I know you miss her now," he said, forcing himself to smile. "But we're doing all right. Maybe if I had a girlfriend, she wouldn't be your mom, but she could help you out with your hair and stuff. She'd be like a big sister."

He lifted up a wooden sculpture from his desk, a carving of a Masai warrior that Mommy bought at a flea market for Daddy's birthday, the year before. She said he was like that warrior. "Strong," she had told my father. "Wooden," she had whispered to me. "Maybe we'll move to Africa," my father said, pacing now, holding the warrior statue sideways in his hand, like a spear. "We could move to Africa and live in a village with all the women fighting to take care of you, to braid that pretty hair. I don't know what we are going to do, princess. But we're going to do something. We're not going to sit here and cry about her leaving. *I'm* not going to cry because she left."

Then he knelt down beside me and rested his head on my lap. His head shook and my hands trembled. I tried to still him. He cried so long that the legs of my pajamas were wet through. At first I wondered if, on top of all the heartbreak of that Christmas, I had peed on myself.

It had taken my father about a month to crack. Part of me suspected that his tears were just another act. I ran my fingers behind my father's ear and collar. There was no hidden tubing, no remote lever for bottled-water tears.

♥

Later that night, I opened my presents. One box held a pair of flared jeans with butterflies stitched on the back pockets. Another box held a white and china blue Holly Hobby tea set. The third box, the biggest one, held a Bubble Yum baby doll that blew her own bubbles. The jeans were too wide-legged. All the cool kids wore Calvin Klein jeans and everybody else wore straight-legged Wranglers, not to mention the teasing I was sure to get for the butterflies on my butt. I wouldn't be caught dead playing with a tea set and I was way too old for baby dolls.

My father watched me open my presents and his eyes flashed like the lights on Jesus' birthday cake as I tore the silver wrapping off of each one. I pretended that I loved them and they were just what I wanted. That night, when my father tucked me into bed, I was hugging Bubble Yum Baby tighter than Linus hangs on to his blanket. My father grazed my cheek with his lips and I smiled.

♥

When my father said that Mommy thought she was a movie star, he meant this revelation to turn me against Mommy. She chose vanity and ambition over us, over me. But I was too young to absorb his accusation. Instead, I began to think of Mommy's leaving in the terms she taught me. When my grandmother died, my mother told me that her own mother had "passed over, into another world." I began to think of Mommy having "passed over," as well. But I did not imagine her in Heaven, I imagined her in Hollywood.

Snowflakes

I dripted through the winter of Mommy's disappearance in flurries of worry and longing. I missed Mommy for all the sweet things she used to do, the way she braided my hair and left me notes for when I came home from school. I also missed her being my father's wife. Life with my father meant taking care of myself and taking care of him too. I learned how to set an alarm clock. I learned how to cook something besides the omelets my father ate with stunning regularity. I learned to remind my father to buy food and how to steal money from his wallet when the reminders went unheeded. I wanted Mommy back not only because I missed the shadow of her womanhood, the way it cloaked me even when she was away at work. I wanted Mommy back because I worried that my father couldn't raise me alone. I knew he wasn't like other fathers with all of his hocus-pocus. But after Mommy left, I realized I'd gotten it all wrong. My father might have been the one in the top hat and tails, the one who stood center stage. But my father wasn't Gladys Knight, he was a Pip.

After school, Daddy tried to keep me busy. I cleaned the bird and rabbit cages, which we kept in the kitchen, and made sure they had enough water. My father owned three doves, which he dyed different colors—red, yellow, and green. They were called Bob Marley, Rita Marley, and Peter Tosh. Peter Tosh was the rude one, who inevitably shit on someone's good suit during a performance. "I love that bird's spirit," Daddy said, chuckling to himself. "But he's headed for the soup pot." The rabbit was a fat, white orb called "the Man" and wasn't much of a playmate. When my mother had been gone for two months, I asked for a dog.

"When was the last time you ever saw a dog in a magic act?" Daddy asked. "I can write off everything I buy to take care of the Man and those birds. They're all business expenses."

"Dogs can do tricks!"

"Stupid pet tricks," Daddy said. "Who would pay to see that?"

Every weekend, I stapled hundreds of color prints of Daddy's head shot to a stack of resumes. "The Amazing Teddo—Seeing Is Disbelieving!" was the tag across the top. Then I put together a folder of letters of appreciation and testimonials to Daddy's talent. "He was the hit of our corporate Christmas party," raved one

Citibank executive. "Months later, our son's friends are still talking about Teddo's performance at his bar mitzvah!" reported another astonished letter writer. Making Daddy's publicity packet was the most boring job in the world, but every week Daddy brought home more boxes of pictures and letters and resumes. "You've got to get your name out there to make it big," he said. "All the magic tricks in the world won't do you a lick of good if folks don't know your name. Harry Blackstone told me that. I met him once at the International Brotherhood of Magicians."

The whole apartment smelled of his lust for fame. "I want to be like Ali," he crooned. "I want them to call me the greatest magician that ever lived." His quest for greatness was like a vase of flowers, scenting the apartment with perpetual waves of bloom and death. For all her fabulousness, Mommy did not like flowers in the house. "They start out pretty," she said, "but they end up smelling of death." On the days when his shows went well, he made a lot of money and could see his big break coming as clear as day, his ambition was sweet and sugared the air. But when a week went by without a booking, he grew, by turns, sullen and furious. He blamed the system. He blamed white people. He blamed Mommy. And though he did not say it, I believed he blamed me. A single man could go west, stake his claim in Las Vegas or L.A. Although he pulled me in and out of schools, like the rabbit from his top hat, my father thought that staying in New York provided some continuity. I prayed that staying in New York meant that Mommy was coming home.

The year before, my mother had given me an art kit for my birthday. I hardly used it before she left. I was too old for coloring and I did not know what to do with the ruler, three pencils with different-sized points, a pen that dipped into a pot of ink. But after my mother left, I tried to write her letters with the ink pot pen but the letters were all the same.

♠

Dear Mommy,
Where are you?

That was it. I never wrote more than one line because that simple sentence reminded me that there was no place to mail the letter once I was done.

One day I was reading a Spider-Man comic, and I started to draw a comic about my mother and my father. In the first panel, there was a picture of my father in a top hat. In the second panel, there was my father, making a hocus-pocus motion with his hand. In the third panel, my mother appeared out of thin air. The pictures weren't very good, but I was proud of myself, the way I copied Sam Rosen's block lettering:

♠♠♠

AND FOR HIS NEXT TRICK, LADIES AND GENTLEMEN,
TEDDO WILL PULL OFF HIS MOST AMAZING FEAT OF ALL.
HE WILL MAKE HIS MISSING WIFE APPEAR. AMAZING!

♠♠♠

I wanted to show my father my comic, but I was afraid of pushing him too far. There was a bright spot in my father's left eye that flashed when he was furious. I saw it focused on bill collectors and on mechanics who kept his precious car too long. The spot flashed when he was reading James Baldwin one day. He threw the book on the floor and I thought he was going to cry. But instead, he went into the kitchen and broke every glass we owned. Then he came into the living room and ordered me to clean up the mess. We drank out of Dixie bathroom cups for a week until he got paid for a show and could buy us some more glasses. I knew my father raged. I did not want him to rage at me.

Daddy worshiped madmen. Doug Henning was a showman, but Houdini was damn well insane. Khia Khan Khruse, a nineteenth-century East Indian magician whom my father revered like a patron saint, kept his guardian angels busy with his unholy attempts at defying mortality. Khruse swallowed pins, then removed them from his eyes. He covered his tongue with boiling wax and then invited stunned audience members to create seals on his taste buds with their signet rings. He ordered a seven-hundred-pound stone to be placed on his chest, then ordered it smashed to pieces with a sledgehammer. Magically, mysteriously, he lived to tell the tale. He was perhaps most well known for his human bull's-eye trick. In England, in 1822, he ordered one terrified British gentleman to aim and shoot a pistol straight at him. Khruse grinned, then in a flash caught the bullet between his fingertips. When my father told me this story he was so in awe, so pleased with Khruse and himself, he actually took a small bow.

Houdini once said that his life as an escape artist was a slap in the face of assimilation. The great magician's father was a Jewish immigrant who came to the land of opportunity and found nothing but closed doors. Houdini decided to make it his life's work to render doors, locks, bolts, and the like meaningless. I believe this is why my father became a magician. For some, the 1960s was an explosion, a revolution, America turned on its axis. For my father, it was too little, too late. He wanted racism to disappear entirely, and when it did not, he decided to make a life's work out of disappearing acts he could control.

By the sixth grade, this is what I knew for sure—that although my father liked to sing along when James Brown screamed, "Say it loud! I'm black and I'm proud," deep inside he felt he was a man born ahead of his time. I knew that the bar mitzvah business was our family's bread and butter, but my father envied the prosperity of the Jews who hired him. My father talked a good game about Afrocentricity, black power, and black pride. But when I saw my father onstage, the way he defied gravity and logic like a colored Houdini, I knew his truth. My father was no freedom fighter. He was simply a man who longed to be free.

"Nothing up my sleeve but elbows," he teased, removing his jacket with a flourish and rolling up the cuffs of his shirt.

Some magicians need to keep a distance. Their magic is only good if they are on a stage. But my father, being black, being the downright uppity Negro that he was, did not rely on the distance of the stage. Like a reverend who is catching the spirit, there came a time in every show when he went to the people. (Have mercy.) When he needed to walk right up to their faces and tell them that seeing is not believing. (Amen.) Because if Pharaoh believed the miracles he saw Moses perform. (Preach it, brother.) Then what? (Amen.) I said, What? (Hallelujah.) He would've let Moses' people go.

My father came down from the stage and into the audience because the applause that came after every trick was not enough for him. He needed to convert the audience from disbelievers to believers, from sinners to suckers. He wanted their applause to be a proclamation. So he invited them to inspect the deck, to inspect his person, to examine his top hat and to tap the floor with his magic cane. Then when he pulled it off—when he picked their card out of the deck, when he pulled a rabbit out of his hat, when he threw his cane into the air and two white doves soared above his head—even the skeptics put their hands together and wondered if my father wasn't part holy man. This was what he loved. This was the glory he was seeking.

♠

Daddy had just finished his set at Chocolate Kiss, a supper club in Queens where he had a regular gig. The food was free, so Daddy brought his whole crew to the show. Uncle Roger was at the bar, Sammy, Daddy, and I were studying the menu.

"It's so rude," I thought I heard Daddy whisper.

"What did you say?" I whispered back.

"It's a dude." He pointed to the woman Uncle Roger was talking to, at the bar.

Sammy, who had been leaning in and trying to stick his straw into my Shirley Temple, started to cackle loudly. My father shot him a dirty look.

"You mean a man?" I whispered, quiet as I could.

Daddy had explained to me that sometimes men fell in love with other men. He said that I would see them in the discos, holding hands and kissing, and that I should make sure not to stare. I got used to seeing gay couples. But the only men I'd ever seen wearing women's clothes were Flip Wilson and Milton Berle on TV. They looked like men trying to be funny. This woman looked more like Jayne Kennedy than Geraldine.

"How do you know?" I asked.

"The scarf around the neck," Daddy said. "It covers up his Adam's apple." He pointed to the bobbing ball in his own neck. "The hands and feet—gigantic."

I couldn't really see it.

A few minutes after the waitress took our order—fried chicken, black-eyed peas, mac and cheese, all around—Uncle Roger came back, looking pleased as punch.

"Teddo, man! Did you see that fox I was rapping to?" Uncle Roger asked. "Her name is Gerri."

"Honey with the scarf?" Daddy said. Then he pointed to his Adam's apple. Uncle Roger looked distraught.

"Nah, man," he said. "It couldn't be. I've got a date with her next week."

Daddy said, "Happens to the best of us, baby. Drinks are on me."

♠

We were halfway through dinner when a white woman came over to our table and sat right down. She flipped her long, dark hair like she was Daisy Duke on the Dukes of Hazzard and she tossed Roger and Sammy a casual "Hey, how you doing, fellas?" She didn't say a word to me.

"Hello, sweetheart," she cooed at my father.

"I thought I asked you to come over later," Daddy said.

"That was an hour ago. I figured this is later."

"This isn't later," Daddy said. "This is now. Later means much later."

She walked around the booth and kissed Daddy on the mouth, long and deep. After she kissed my father smack dab on the lips, she turned to me and asked, "So what's your name, little girl?" as if she were Santa Claus and I was sitting on her lap.

"If you're kissing my father like that, you should know my name," I answered, rolling my eyes like Florence on *The Jeffersons*.

Sammy laughed so hard that he spit his drink through his nose, which only made him laugh harder. "I guess she told you," he kept saying over and over again. "Uh-huh, don't mess with our girl. 'Cause Miss Angela will read you."

Roger just chuckled, a laugh deep and soft. He was wearing a brown-and-yellow silk shirt and his head was shaved clean. He'd taken his aviator sunglasses off when she came over to the table. It seemed, at first, to be a gesture of politeness. But I could tell by the way he kept giving her the bouncer's eye that he thought she was trouble.

Daddy did not laugh, but he didn't seem annoyed at me either. He slouched back in the chair, in a laid-back repose that was so uncharacteristic that it put me on edge.

"Angela, I want you to meet Dana," he said.

Dana put out her hand. "Pleased to meet you, Angela," she said in the same fake friendly voice a telephone operator uses to say the same thing a hundred times a day. "My friends call me Danita."

"Danita?" I repeated, blankly. What kind of white woman is named Danita? And when did Daddy start sleeping with the enemy?

Danita was skinny in a way that seemed to suggest both poverty and a certain kind of wealth. Her shoulders jutted out of her silvery tube top. She had no breasts to speak of, and I imagined that the tube top was held up, on the inside, with Scotch tape.

Her skin was not the pale pink of Barbie dolls, but greenish white with patches of red dots near her mouth and on her arms. She wore braces, which seemed strange to me. I'd never seen a grown woman with braces. Her eye shadow was an unsettling melange of purple and gold. In magazines, the style made the model's eyes look like a tiger's stripe—sexy and wild. Danita looked like she'd gone face first into a door, then stepped back and repeated the trick with the other eye. She had no lips, just a slash of red indicated the space where her mouth opened and words came out. To say I didn't like her was wrong.

As I dissected her hair, her body, her skin, what I felt more than anything was shock. How could Daddy choose to kiss this woman? She was no replacement for Mommy. My beautiful mother with her smooth cherrywood skin, full lips, and and round hips. That Mommy was beautiful was scientific fact. When we used to walk down the street, we were followed by catcalls. "Can I get some fries to go with that shake, cutie?" the guys on the corner called out. When they asked Mommy how she was doing, she replied, "Fine, thank you." Which prompted the inevitable comeback of "I can see you fine, sexy. I asked how are you doing?" In comparison to my Foxy Brown mommy, Danita was beat-up-after-school ugly. Not to mention, she was batting for the wrong team.

I tried to come up with an explanation as I slurped my ginger ale with grenadine, then studiously tried to lift each of three cherries out of the glass with a straw. When it became clear that I was slurping from an empty cup, Danita grabbed the glass away from me.

"I know what you're thinking," she said, hissing across the table. "You're wondering what your daddy's doing with a white woman. Well, let me tell you something, I am not white, I am light-skinned!"

Her voice was loud and sharp and shocking. Unlike the other women who tried to charm my father, she seemed to have no desire to get on my good side. Roger was right. Trouble, for sure. But what was stranger still was the way she said the words. She spread them out, in a ghetto pronunciation. "Light skin-ded." I just stared. Mistaking my silence for deafness, she squealed her proclamation again. "*I am light skin-ded!*" she said.

Sammy was sprawled across the banquette. He couldn't stop

laughing. His polyester disco shirt was stained with sweat and I could see the rings under his arms as he beat the vinyl seat with his arms. "This is some shit," he said, rolling. "This is some truly funny shit."

"I know what y'all call me—snowflake," Danita said. "I ain't no snowflake. I got more soul than all you bougie-ass brothers rolled into one."

Daddy seemed to have heard enough. "I'm going to take Angela home, Danita," he said as he stood. "It's way past her bedtime. Let me walk you to your car."

Danita took a swig of what she was drinking, then stood, wobbly and uneven. "You don't have to walk me to my car, Teddo," she said. "I'm not your child. I don't have a bedtime, nigga!"

Light skin-ded or not, she'd crossed the line and everybody at the table knew it. There were five seconds of pure frightening silence, like in those old Western movies when the picture slows to show the sheriff reaching for his gun.

I heard Roger mutter under his breath, "Good Lord in heaven, have mercy."

Daddy's eyes were bulging and his fists were locked around Danita's bony arms like manacles. I could see him push her through the crowd on the dance floor and seconds later, Roger was on his feet. "Stupid bitch. I better make sure he doesn't hurt her," he said to no one in particular. Then he turned to Sammy, "Keep an eye on Angela."

"I've got both my eyes on Miss Angela," Sammy said.

"And if she needs to go to the bathroom . . ."

Sammy cut him off. "Yeah, yeah. If she needs to go to the bathroom, I should come and get Teddo."

Sammy poured half of his drink into my glass.

"What's this?" I asked, before I tasted it.

"It's got orange juice in it," he said, his eyes swimming behind his glasses, like goldfish in a bowl. "And just a little bit of vodka. You'll like it. It's sweet."

I drank it in one gulp. Then Sammy refilled my glass.

"It'll help you get to sleep tonight," he said, still laughing to himself. "Forget about all this drama."

"Your eyes are red, Sammy," I said, moving closer to his face.

"So are yours."

"Really?"

Sammy smiled. "Do the words 'contact high' mean anything to you, Ange?"

"Nope."

"Don't worry, they will," Sammy giggled.

"What does it mean?" I asked, annoyed that he was laughing at me.

"Ask your dad," he said.

"Don't worry, I will," I said, in the snidest voice I could muster.

"You got a boyfriend, Angela?"

"No" is what I said. But I was thinking, Sammy is so stupid. There would be ice-skating in hell before one of the boys at school noticed me.

"You want a boyfriend?"

I didn't answer him. I was staring at the dance floor; Gerri was dancing with a big tough guy who looked a little like James Earl Jones.

"I really don't think he's your type."

"Who?"

"Mr. Gerri," Sammy said, cracking himself up again.

He paused then and looked at me as if trying to determine whether I could keep a secret. "Angela, baby, let me ask you something."

"Sure."

"You know how folks are always saying, 'Underneath we're all the same'?"

I nodded.

"It's not true. Beneath the skin, we're all different. That's what makes it so goddamn hard."

"What, Sammy? What's so hard?" Sammy was rarely philosophical. That was my dad's territory. In my father's court, he was the king, Roger was the wise man, and Sammy was the court jester.

"Nothing sweetheart," Sammy said, looking sad. "Drink a little more."

I drank up and felt myself getting sleepy, just like Sammy said. I kicked my shoes off, then sat cross-legged on the leather banquette.

"So is she really black?" I asked Sammy.

"Hell no," he answered, with a smirk.

How Men Mother

One afternoon at school, the nurse said my fever was too high and that my father should come get me. I panicked.

"Can I just lie down in the infirmary?" I pleaded, making helpless little girl eyes at her. She was Caribbean and I immediately fell in love with the music she made every time she opened her mouth. Like so many of the island women in our Brooklyn neighborhood, she was round and soft in ways that suggest warmth. Yet these women, I knew, were capable of a colonial strictness that was icy cold. The nurse's response was a mild autumn breeze. "You will be far more comfortable in your own bed," she sang-spoke at me.

I did not want my father to come because he did not respond well to sickness. The summer before, Daddy got a booking to do a harvest festival in Bucks County, Pennsylvania. We drove four hours each way. At the festival, Daddy did a strolling magician act and I soon became bored following him. I asked him for a dollar, to buy a corndog. I'd never tasted one before. He gave it to me and the dog was delicious. I went back and asked him for another dollar, then another dollar. By the time we drove home, I'd eaten five and was sick to the gills.

"I think I'm going to vomit," I whispered.

"Speak up!" my father ordered, in his favorite preacher voice. "The black people of the world have been silent too long!"

"Daddy," I said, raising my voice like a rabbit peeking his head above a top hat. "I think I'm going to be sick."

My father slammed on the brakes, hopped out of the car, and opened up the passenger door. Just in time for me to vomit all over his Ferragamo shoes. Cars sped by us and I could hear all kinds of critters in the bushes. But the world was oddly still and frightening because my father did not say a word.

My hands were covered with vomit because I'd tried to hold the sickness back and I was on my knees because I'd kind of stumbled out of the car. I was kneeling before my father then, my hands outstretched with the evidence of my shame. Even then, my position seemed religious. That day, on the side of the road, he stared at me with a look so menacing, so disgusted, I did not doubt I'd be turned to stone.

"Wait for me here," he said, finally. His voice was thick and gravelly.

My back was turned to the car and I did not witness his departure. I heard my father's shoes on the sandy road; his weight pressing down loudly on each little stone. The pounding turned to a crackling, then all I heard was the sound of a pebble being kicked away in the distance before the engine revved and he was gone. It's a sad sound the road makes when a man walks away from you. Especially when he is your father and you are not entirely sure that he is coming back.

The heavy door of my father's German car shut with gravity. When I heard the engine start, I burst into tears. My father did not roll the window down to say, "I'll get help, baby," or even to repeat his earlier instructions. The car started, the wheels kicked back dirt, and he spun away.

I waited until I was sure he was gone to turn and gaze at the empty road behind me. I saw that a few feet away from the tire marks, my father had left his shoes, drenched in my vomit.

I did not own a watch and I had no sense of time. I want to tell you that he was gone for hours and that it began to rain, that the sun lowered itself out of the sky and I was left in darkness. I want to tell you that a nice older couple in a pickup truck slowed down and rescued me. I fantasized about a kind woman running me a bath, giving me some fizzy powder to settle my stomach, then waiting with me by the road until my father returned.

What I figure is that my father was gone for about half an hour. Not more than forty minutes, though it felt like forty years. He returned with two rolls of paper towels in hand. One roll was sopping wet and sat in a shopping bag. The other was new, still wrapped in plastic with the orange convenience store price still stuck on it. My father opened the trunk of the car and gave me a bag of new clothes: a pink-and-yellow T-shirt that seemed too girly for both my taste and my father's. There was also a floral skirt.

I took the clothes and the two rolls of paper towel and headed into the bushes in the direction my father pointed. When I was clean and dressed, we left the dirty clothes by the side of the road and drove away. The whole way home, my father barely said a word. He was wearing new shoes.

Too long a story to tell the pretty nurse. Her name was Miss Chase and I noticed that she was not wearing a wedding ring. Maybe my father would like her. Maybe she could come and be my mother.

"You have a fever of a hundred and one," she said scientifically. "That is unacceptable. I not only want your father to take you home, you must go to a doctor as well."

I knew full well that the magicians' union—if there was such a thing—did not provide health insurance. Doctors meant bills. Bills put my father in a foul mood.

"If you have some ice cubes, I could suck on them and it might bring my fever down," I offered. The walls of the nurse's office were light green, like hospital scrubs.

"Little girl," Nurse Chase said sternly, holding my face in her hands. Her red talons pressed into my cheeks, her brown eyes were blazing. "You are sick and ice cubes are not medicine. What's your problem, child? Most children love to get a day off from school."

"It's just that my father is very busy. I hate to bother him."

"What about your mother? Is she working?"

I looked away and willed my eyes to fill with tears. To keep the nurse from calling my father, I needed to play the scene to full effect.

"I-I-I," I stammered. "I don't have a mother!" I threw my head onto my folded arms, squeezing my eyes tight to keep the tears coming.

She didn't embrace me and I was more than a little disappointed. "I see" was all she said as she lifted an index card with our home number on it and dialed my dad.

When he arrived, I was lying on the bed in the examining room. But I could tell from their extended conversation that he liked her and she liked him. I heard her chuckle softly and when she squealed with surprise, I knew that he'd pulled a quarter from her ear. I did not know where the liking led. My father did not bring women to our apartment and they did not call the house. But I suspected that he spent time with them after his shows, those evenings when he was late coming home to me.

◆

We got into the car and my father drove away from the school. For a few minutes, I thought he was really taking me to the doctor. But he was just in petulant schoolboy mode, waiting for us to be out of the nurse's earshot because he turned to me and asked, "So, how sick are you?"

"Well, I have a fever," I said, pressing the back of my hand to my own forehead.

My father touched my forehead, then my throat, then my wrist as if to check that I still had a pulse. "You're kind of warm," he said. "But you look okay to me. Do you have to vomit?"

"Nope," I said with confidence.

"Good," he said. "Then why don't you stay home for a couple of days and watch TV? If you're still not feeling well by the end of the week, maybe that nice nurse will make a house call."

My father drove me home and set me up on his bed. "Since you're sick," he said. "I'll sleep in your room and you can sleep in mine. There's a bigger bed and you can watch TV." He went to the grocery store and I settled in to watch all the shows that he did not usually let me see, subversive suburban propaganda like *The Brady Bunch* and *The Partridge Family*. My father said the sooner I learned not to pull the foolhardy stunts that white kids did, the better. He drummed it into my head that black kids were killed for a lot less than the petty shoplifting, cheating, and lying that were at the center of those sitcom morality plays. "Emmett Till was lynched for whistling at a white woman," he growled. "You remember that when you're watching *Eight Is Enough*."

When my father left, I crawled out of bed and dragged myself to the bathroom. I spit into the sink and rinsed my mouth. I was so afraid of being sick in my father's bed that I made frequent trips to the bathroom where I brought up nothing more than a mouthful of spit. My father's suit from the night before was bunched in a corner near the bathroom door. It lay there, oversized and sloppy, like a scarecrow had just undressed. I put my father's jacket on over my turquoise blue long johns. It was sunset orange, with satin lapels. I couldn't have clashed more—the bright blue waffle pattern of my pajama top peeking through the suit jacket. But when I closed my eyes and pressed my cheek against the velvety soft shoulder, it was all I could do not to lose myself.

The jacket smelled of dark and smoky places. My clothes smelled that way too, when I went to clubs with my father. Underneath the top note, there was the mixed-together smell of all my father used to get clean: soap, aftershave, cocoa butter lotion, Right Guard deodorant, Afro Sheen for his hair. At the bottom, there was the smell of near-fresh sweat.

I took the jacket off and threw it back on the pile of dirty clothes. I was starting to gain a new appreciation for a messy apartment. I was starting to like the dirty clothes on the floor, the unwashed dishes in the sink. It all had the air of unfinished business, and unfinished business felt like nobody was leaving.

When he returned from the grocery store, my father glanced at the television but didn't say a word. He prepared a tray for me of corn flakes, Coca-Cola, and ice cream. When I stuck my spoon into the cereal bowl, I noticed that the milk was icy. I lifted the cube with my spoon and held it out before him. He had climbed into bed next to me and was eating cereal too.

"You've got a fever," he said. "You need to have cold things."

On the bed in front of my father sat a chess set, each piece made of a dark, carved wood, a gift from one of his clients. We used the mysterious, thickly cut pieces to play checkers with, jumping horses over pawns and rooks over queens. Royalty held no sway and when one piece made it safely across the board and someone shouted out, "King me!" we relied on memory to remind us that a pawn or a knight was really a king.

On that first full day of school I missed, we played checkers. As always, he was black and I was white. "The black man shall be triumphant!" he said. And I wondered where that left the black woman. Five minutes into the game, I carelessly let him double jump two of my pawns.

"What were you thinking?" my father asked, annoyed at the easy win.

I shrugged. "I don't know," I said. "I just moved."

My father grabbed my wrist. "Don't do that," he said. "Never just play. Think about what you're doing or don't waste my time."

"It's just a game," I insisted.

"That's not the way white people do it," my father said, shaking his head. "It's never just a game with them. Look at how they play sports. Look at how they do Muhammad Ali, look at how they trash-talk Reggie Jackson."

He went into the bathroom and came back with an old copy of *Sports Illustrated*. "Look at this magazine and tell me who's the most famous athlete in the world."

I just read what was in front of me. "Terry Bradshaw. The Regulator."

"Fuck Terry Bradshaw!" Daddy said. "I'd give Terry Bradshaw

five dollars if he could regulate his own bowel movements. Pelé is the most important athlete in the world. The man stopped a civil war."

"Is he a soldier?" I glanced at the clock, wondering how long this particular rant might last.

"Hell no. He's a soccer player. The greatest soccer player in the world."

"I've never heard of him."

"Of course you haven't," Daddy said, shaking his head and looking at me sadly, wondering how to cure me of my ignorance. "That's because I'm raising you in the belly of the racist beast. Americans only want to talk about football because soccer is a game that colored people rule. Do you hear me?"

I nodded.

"Then repeat after me," Daddy said, energetic now, dazzling and alive in that place between madness and passion, the place he called home.

"Soccer is a game that colored people rule," he began.

"Soccer is a game that colored people rule!" I said, throwing my imaginary pompoms out like a Dallas Cowboy cheerleader.

"By colored people, I don't just mean black people. I mean Indian people and Hispanic people and all those white people that the white people can't stand. Like the Irish and the Italians. They got some Italians who are darker than me. You have no idea, Angela. No idea."

I fiddled with my queen on the chessboard, tapping it ever so slightly.

"Pelé won the world championships and I couldn't even watch it on American TV. Terry Bradshaw throws a lame-ass pass and it's prime time. Can't seem to find a black man to play quarterback, though they loved them some Joe Namath. Even gave him a talk show, a platform for his nonexistent ideas. It's never just a game, baby. When you are black like us, you've got to think about your every move."

"If the game is so important," I asked, feeling bold in my special status as patient, "why do we play checkers with this chess set? If we're so smart, why don't we play chess?"

My father paused a moment and then hugged me tightly. "You are absolutely right. The black man has to learn how to play chess. I'm going to go to the library and get us a book."

♦

The next day we played chess, the elegant pieces taking on new dimensions as we learned their true names and the physics of how they were able to move. I liked the way the bishops slid diagonally across the board—once the pawns were out of their way—as fast and as far as they could go. I imagined them, bearded old men on skateboards, their long velvet robes brushing the sidewalk floor. Daddy loved the way the knights moved, one step forward and two steps sideways. "It's like magic," he said, beaming. "It's all about misdirection. It's Kareem Abdul-Jabbar, dribbling towards a basket, evading the other team's defense. You've got to bob and weave in chess, I dig that."

We played, badly, stumbling like toddlers. So mostly, my father did what he did best: he told me fables and tall tales. My favorite was the story of the human chess game in Venice that decided the fate of a young couple in love. The year was 1454 and the most powerful man in the city was Taddeo Parisio, rector of Marostica. When I pointed out that Teddo and Taddeo were nearly identical names, Daddy grinned and gave me a wink. "Maybe he was an ancestor of mine," he said cheerfully, dropping his race rhetoric in an unexpected show of good humor. He pointed to the skin on his arm, so many shades lighter than my own, and said, "I knew there was some milk in my coffee. Maybe old Taddeo was in the mix.

"Taddeo, Mr. Big Stuff, the Mack Daddy of Venice, had two beautiful daughters," Daddy continued. "Be happy you don't have a sister, Angela. When there's two beautiful daughters, there's always somebody stirring the pot. Remind me to tell you, someday, about King Lear."

I rolled my eyes and pulled sick-girl privilege, "Keep going, Daddy."

As the story goes, there are two men in love with Lionora, the oldest daughter. Secretly, she loves only one of them back. Custom dictates that she can't choose her suitor. Both men are born into nobility; either pairing would add prestige and honor to the Parisio family name. Since neither man will abandon his affection, they vow to settle the matter in a gentlemanly fashion. They will duel to the death.

Taddeo Parisio is a peaceful man. He does not want his daughter's matrimonial home built on a field of blood. He goes to his daughter's suitors, Rinaldo d'Angarano and Vieri da Vallonara, and offers up a more sporting proposal. The two men, both known to be excellent players, will battle in a game of chess. The winner will marry Lionora. The defeated will marry her younger sister, Oldrada.

The region ignites with the news of Taddeo's Solomonic solution. It will be a great game followed by an engagement feast for the betrothed daughters. Lionora is still not appeased. Her lover's life is no longer at risk, but perhaps this is worse. If he loses she will have to see him every day, married to her sister, and she will be forced to call him brother instead of husband.

The day of the match, the courtyard is covered with a human-sized board. Taddeo announces his conceit—the palace servants will serve as pieces. The players will direct their pieces to move from high chairs which have been constructed on opposite ends of the board. The game begins at dusk.

Lionora, afraid that her face will betray her, watches from a window overlooking the courtyard. She has confided her affections, though not the name of her beloved, to one person—her handmaiden, who watches the game from the crowd. She tells her maid that if her love should win, she will light a candle in her bedroom window as a message to her beloved of her joy.

The game goes on for hours. Peasants dressed as pawns are toppled. Playacting, forfeited pieces feign dramatic deaths as they slump to the ground, then scurry away. Mistakes are made and powerful pieces are lost. Rinaldo foolishly parts with a rook. Vieri, heartbroken, sacrifices a knight. The game goes on so long that it seems the stars themselves will topple out of the sky before either player captures the opposing king. Then it happens. Vieri successfully negotiates a difficult bishop ending and wins Lionora's hand.

The engagements are announced. Vieri to Lionora. Rinaldo to Oldrada. Music is played and a feast is served. The dancing lasts well into the night. Close to morning the last guest goes home and the family—proud father, promised daughters—goes to bed. The servants begin the work of straightening all that the evening's festivities have put awry. Then the handmaiden sees it. A light burning in Lionora's window. From servant to servant, the secret is whispered, an order to look skyward and the reason why.

My father, voracious for knowledge, hungry for the passion that chess incites, read me all kinds of chess stories as I lay in my sickbed. He especially loved reading accounts of the 1972 Fischer versus Spassky world championship match. He marveled at how Fischer conjured the spirit of the board, raining down terror like he was the crankily awakened king of the damned. "Bobby Fischer is Houdini reincarnated," Daddy said, offering the great chess master his highest praise.

The story of Lionora, however, remained my favorite: the one I asked my father to read to me repeatedly that week when I was home sick and even after, when my fever passed and I was well enough to read to myself. Of course, I saw myself as Lionora and Mommy as the suitor to whom I could not confess my love. For days, I dreamed myself into the fairy tale, imagining Lionora's candle as a beacon, a lighthouse to bring Mommy safely to shore. An impossible plan. Even if I had the money to buy a candle. Even if I could burn it without my father noticing the smell or the light. How could Mommy see it, unless she was standing right under our brownstone window to see it. If she was so close, what was the use? Mommy was a lion and I was her cub. If she was close enough to see the candle, she need not rely on sight to know that I was near. Her tongue would sting with the salt of my tears. Her powerful nose would detect the sour smell of my sweat as I slept bundled in my bed. She would hear, from a mile away if not farther, the sound of my heart beating and if she could, she would come, knocking down doors if she needed to. But she did not come that winter. I consoled myself by making up my own chess stories. Chess is a difficult game to win without your queen, but a game without a king is no game at all.

My father took good care of me that week. He brought my meals in on a tray. During the day, we played chess. Daytime talk shows droned in the background: Mike Douglas, Phil Donahue, Dinah Shore. On Saturday, we watched cartoons and old Charlie Chaplin movies on channel five. On Sunday, we watched Gil Noble telling the truth and shaming the devil on *Like It Is*. In the evening, Daddy tried out new magic tricks and read me passages from Haile Selassie and Khalil Gibran until I fell asleep. And because my father believed that you must freeze a fever, I ate obscene amounts of ice cream

The following Tuesday, when he took my temperature and got 98.6 degrees, he asked me how I felt.

"Much better," I said. "I'd like to go to school tomorrow."

"Good, Angela, I'm glad," he said, kissing me on the cheek. "See you in the morning."

And for the first time since Mommy left, I thought, Maybe he can do this. Maybe we can be a family all by ourselves.

♦

On Valentine's Day, my father gave me a box of chocolates—a Whitman's sampler—and told me to make sure I was dressed by the time he came home. It was seven in the morning, but Daddy dragged me out of bed, went over to the stereo, and put on a reggae album.

"Tonight, I'm taking my best girl out," he said. We were going to Ecstasy, one of Daddy's favorite discos.

We danced to the music the way my father taught me: swaying to the slow, island rhythms, each step exaggerated like an astronaut walking on the moon. On the record player, a dreamy voice sang "Redemption Song."

I carried the box of chocolates to school that day, confident it would attract the attention I hoped for. I waited for someone to ask me for a piece, offering me the opportunity to strike up a conversation. Walking to school, I imagined a rumor starting that some boy gave the chocolates to me. If anyone asked, I planned to say they were from my boyfriend from my old school who'd brought them by the house the day before. I'd dressed carefully for the day, brushing my hair until it lay flat, combing out my baby hair. I put Vaseline on my lips and wore my favorite cream sweater and my best pair of jeans. But no one commented on my clothes or the chocolates.

At lunchtime some of the girls passed out store-bought Valentines to their friends, but no one asked about my chocolates. After lunch, I took the box out of my bag and tried resting it on top of my books. Then I turned the words face out, so the other kids could read what the box said. I even tried dropping my history book on the floor to get people to look. But all that happened was the teacher told me to stop fidgeting. She didn't even say, "I hope you brought enough for the whole class, Angela," because as a matter of fact, I did. It was a big box, forty-eight pieces. When I came home from school, I still had the same forty-eight pieces. I stood in front of our door, counting the rows of chocolates. Then I quickly put six pieces in my mouth all at once, just in case my father was home and just in case he noticed.

♦

That night, at Ecstasy, I was sitting in a booth with Sammy, waiting for Daddy to come out after his show. A honey-toned woman with blond braids sauntered over to our table.

"What's happening, Sammy?" she said. "Where's Teddo?"

Sammy gave her an approving look. "You looking good, Diana. Teddo's finishing up backstage. Have a seat, baby girl."

She squeezed into the booth next to us. Her skin seemed to glimmer against the banquette.

"Who's this darling little girl?" she asked.

"This is Angela, Teddo's daughter."

"Aren't you the prettiest thing I've ever seen?" she said, and I instantly took a dislike to her. I wasn't bothered by what she said, it was the sticky-sweet baby voice she used. There was usually some woman trying to talk to my father when we went to the clubs. He seemed interested, but I didn't see the same woman twice. No one—not me, not Daddy, not Uncle Roger or Sammy—ever mentioned that my mother may have been gone, but my father was still, very much, a married man.

I gave her a two-second smile that showed no teeth.

"Where's Teddo with his fine self?" she asked, looking around. Then she turned to me and said, "Your daddy's got that good hair."

"Oh really? How do you define good?" I said, just the way Daddy taught me. He hated when people talked about good hair and bad hair. I knew he wasn't going to like it when I told him that this woman started with that mess.

My father came over and his face brightened when he saw Diana. "Hey, lady, it's been a while."

"You know me, Teddo," Diana said. "I'm never gone for too long."

"Let me buy you a drink," Daddy said, and he escorted her away from the table and over to the bar. I waited, anxiously, for him to come back.

♦

Daddy told me not to use the bathrooms in the club. I was only allowed to use the employee bathroom in the back and only when he checked it first and stood guard in front of the door. I didn't understand the fuss, I just figured it was because the club bathrooms were filthy. Daddy was funny like that; our house was a mess, but he was mighty disdainful about germs and dirt in public places.

I waited for Daddy to come back from the bar. But he was taking an awfully long time and I needed to pee.

"I'm going to the bathroom," I told Sammy.

"Okay, sweetie," he said.

I cut across the dance floor, eye-to-armpit with the throngs of disco dancers. Walking across was like swimming through a sea of silky brown bellies and swiveling hips. I kept wanting to touch the plumage that strutted past me—was the leopard print as velvety as the back of a puppy's ear? Were the icy rhinestones that criss-crossed belts and boots and necklines cool to the touch? Were the leather pants smooth or rough? Without being able to see faces, the dance floor was a blind man's zoo. I wanted to wander through it, arms outstretched.

I couldn't reach the toilet fast enough. I rushed into one of the two pink stalls, my eyes quickly taking in the graffiti: curses and phone numbers. I locked the door, hoisted myself high above the seat, and peed. When I opened the door, I could see into the stall across from me. There was a woman on her knees, wedged between the wall and the toilet, quickly sniffing something off the back of the toilet tank. She was dressed in red satin short shorts and a matching mesh top. Her legs went on forever, wrapped like barber poles in red-and-white tights. She was wearing roller skates.

I stepped back into the toilet to watch her. If she heard me, she didn't turn around. I kept thinking, "I've got to wash my hands." But there was something about her wearing skates that made me feel that if I tried to leave, she'd zoom over and catch me. I stood in the toilet stall, waiting for her to finish or close her door, except she never did. She fell backward and began to shake and vomit. I should have gotten help, but my mind was a flurry of thoughts. If she was hurting, why didn't she scream? If I tried to run past her, would she grab my legs and pull me down? She was now sprawled across the bathroom floor and I didn't know if I was brave enough to step over her. I couldn't decide which scared me more, staying or leaving.

I counted to three and made an exaggerated leap over the woman. I ran out of the bathroom and smack dab into Daddy, who was pissed.

"I thought I told you—" he began.

"There's a woman in the bathroom. She's sick," I told him, shaking from the memory. "She was sniffing something off the back of the toilet then she fell and started to vomit. She's wearing roller skates."

Daddy ordered me not to move. He whistled for Roger, who got the bouncer. A few seconds later, the bouncer, a muscle-bound giant, emerged from the bathroom with the woman, slumped over his broad shoulder. Then he carried her away, her candy-cane legs flopped over his back. She looked like she was a raggedy doll. Her skates seemed to keep time to the music. Daddy and Roger followed him through the lines of people doing the bus stop and once again, Daddy growled, "Don't move."

But I didn't listen. Eyes open or eyes closed, all I could see was that woman's face, her snot and her vomit, and her shaking. I made my way onto the dance floor and buried myself in the middle of the crowd where no one could see me. When Michael Jackson started singing, "We're the party people night and day / Living crazy that's the only way," my eyes filled with tears. I cried harder and danced harder until my arms ached and my legs barely held me up. A mirror ball sparkled high above me and I reached up to touch it, but the diamonds of light spun like a firefly right out of my hand. As loud as the music was, I could still hear the sound of the woman's snorting: a harsh, scratchy sound like nails and water in a rusty drain. Then the symphony of bodies around me stopped spinning; two legs in front of me did not move. I looked up to see my father, who did not say a word. He lifted me up in a single scoop and carried me all the way home, where I closed my eyes, but did not sleep.

The Candy Store Is Calling You

Em**b**a**rr**a**ss**ed at not ever having been to college, my father filled our house with books. Daddy had neither the money nor patience to attend college and his lack of formal education plagued him. Without it, he feared that he could never be what he dreamed of: a Great Man. A leader of the people. An entry under *B* in the Encyclopedia of Black History's onion-thin pages. He did not read most of the books he owned, but they comforted him in a way. The way some people keep images of Christ around them, the books were totems of my father's faith that the wrongs inflicted on black people could be made right by book learning. Just as the coming of Christ was predicted in scripture, Daddy felt the glory days of black people were heralded in books: from Frederick Douglass's *Narrative of the Life of Frederick Douglass, An American Slave* to W. E. B. Du Bois's *The Souls of Black Folk* to *The Autobiography of Malcolm X*.

I can picture my father's books as easily as I can picture my father's friends. Alongside Uncle Roger and Sammy, I can see Frantz Fanon seething behind his black skin and white mask. I can see the raised fist of Stokely Carmichael's *Black Power*, and I can picture Chancellor Williams, dressed in khakis, an archaeologist at the dig of my father's soul, every time my father picked up *The Destruction of Black Civlization*. I was taught to question my white teachers and the history lessons I was given in school by Lerone Bennett Jr.'s *Before the Mayflower*. H. Rap Brown shaped my father's anger into poetry, smooth, supple words that filled his heart with pride. The poetry made my father float on air and, in turn, he took me along for the ride. My father is the only man I know who can make whole passages of *Die Nigger Die* sound like a love song.

Daddy fancied himself a public intellectual and a progressive. This was, I knew even then, a slightly skewed take on the term since "up" with Daddy didn't mean "up with the people." Still, he viewed his life as a one-man movement: if only he could get it right, it would change the world. Every plan was grandiose. Every gesture, over the top.

Every six months he came up with a new scheme for intellectual ascendance. The last one took the shape of French lessons—given on twelve cassettes Daddy bought at a used book store.

Doubtlessly, the previous owner of the tapes hoped to travel one day to Paris to order, without embarrassment, *"Un café et un croque monsieur"* at Les Deux Magots on the boulevard St-Germain. Daddy was far more ambitious. He reckoned that fluency in French could position him to be the ambassador to Senegal, a country Daddy had become obsessed with since Mommy brought home our first Youssou N'dour album. "Twelve lessons isn't enough to actually conduct diplomatic business," Daddy admitted when Mommy grimaced at the thirty dollars Daddy paid for the tapes. "But it's a start."

There was, we learned, a distinguished legacy of black ambassadors. In 1949 Truman sent one Edward R. Dudley to Liberia, in West Africa. He was followed by Eisenhower appointees Jessie D. Locker and Richard L. Jones. And while Daddy applauded Kennedy for having the guts to appoint a black ambassador to Europe, he wasn't interested in going to what he called the White Continent. "They can keep it," Daddy said, shaking his head as if ambassadorial posts were being offered to him left and right. "I don't want to go to Italy or Sweden or, God forbid, Germany. Send me to Africa. Send me to my people."

Mommy just rolled her eyes. "Your people? What do you really know about Africa, Teddo?" she said. "Who do you think sold us into slavery, all those years ago? Wasn't the white man that could make his way through the jungle, take sleeping babies out of their beds. Black men led the way, pocketed the profits. Don't you read any of those books that you buy? Look at how they treated Andrew Young! The Africans didn't trust him. Said he was a house Negro."

Daddy's warm, throaty laugh melted Mommy's cold words. He jumped from his chair and stood behind her. He put his arms around her shoulders and swayed her from side to side. "Let it go, Melanie," he said. "All that hatred. Let it go! All that negativity. Where does it come from, baby?" Then he began to kiss the side of her neck, so softly it made me dreamy. He looked like a gentle man.

"You're a damn fool, do you know that, Teddo?" Mommy said, her soft purr taking all the meanness out of the words.

"As long as you're my queen, I don't care," Daddy said, turning on the charm. "I don't mind being a fool as long as you'll be my queen of fools."

Mommy didn't say a word, she just laid her head into Daddy's chest and the two of them rocked slowly to music I could not hear.

By week's end, Daddy involved us in his scheme. My job was to learn how to curtsy. "I thought the curtsy was a British thing," Mommy said as Daddy mimicked a little girl holding the hem of her skirt; I curtsied alongside him. Daddy didn't even turn to answer the question. "It's not a British thing," he said, holding on to his imaginary skirt. "It's a polite thing. It's a sign of manners and good breeding around the world." I practiced my curtsy until my knees ached. Then Daddy decided to teach me how to serve drinks on a tray.

"We'll have servants, of course," Daddy said. "But sometimes at those Connecticut parties that I work at, the little girls serve drinks to their parents' friends. It's really cute." For an hour, I balanced four full glasses of water on the top of a plastic TV tray. I walked around the apartment in my purple Easter dress and my black leather church shoes, the ones with the tiny little heel, asking imaginary guests, "May I offer you a cocktail? Perhaps a martini?" Neither Mommy or Daddy drank anything but beer. Daddy assured us though that once he became an ambassador, martinis would be on the menu every night.

I wasn't the only one with a curriculum. While Daddy practiced his French tapes, Mommy was to learn the business of hostessing. Daddy came back from the used book store with a beat-up copy of Emily Post. "Teddo, this book is more than fifty years old," Mommy said. She wore green velvet pants and a black turtleneck. She was just back from the hairdresser and her hair was feathered to perfection. She'd come home feeling gorgeous and now Daddy was running his mouth about what some old white lady could teach her about being a woman. He was asking for it, but he was also up to the task.

"Good manners never go out of style, Mel," Daddy said, his voice a warm breeze blowing Mommy's way. I didn't need to look up to know that Mommy wasn't feeling my father's game.

"I've got manners," Mommy said. "I don't need no siddity white woman to tell me how to behave." She held the book up, looking at the back-cover picture disparagingly.

"That's Emily Post; she wrote the book on manners," Daddy said, putting on his sweet voice. "It'll be a lot different when you're serving state dinners to fifty guests at a time, honey. Just see what the book has to say."

Daddy took the book from Mommy and opened it to the chapter on setting a table. "You make a lovely table," my father said, pointing to the dining room table Mommy covered with African cloth. "But this here is just a reference book. When I get the call to take the diplomat's test, you'll be tested too. They'll come to our house and want to see how you set the table."

"Hmmph," Mommy snorted. "I know how to set a damn table."

My father flipped through the book. "But Mel, do you know how to set a table like this? With all these spoons and forks?"

Mommy glanced sideways at the book and shrugged.

"I need you, baby," my father said. "I need you to learn how to set a formal table."

So Mommy did. I helped her. We didn't have enough silverware or plates to copy the picture, but we used plastic forks and knives and paper plates to fill the empty places. We began each evening with the plates, spaced around the table at equal distances. Emily Post suggested a tape measure, but Mommy insisted we could eyeball it. Forks went to the left: salad fork, meat fork, then fish fork. Mommy said she hadn't heard of a fish fork, or serving meat and fish in the same meal. But Daddy, who sat on the couch listening to his French tapes, insisted that at state dinners, both meat and fish were served.

"Some people are vegetarians," he pointed out.

"Then they wouldn't eat meat or fish," Mommy countered.

"Some kinds of vegetarians only eat fish," Daddy insisted.

"Yeah, sure," Mommy said. "The trifling kind."

Knives went to the right, in the same order: meat knife, then fish knife, then soup spoon. Mommy said we could skip the oyster fork and grapefruit spoon as we weren't likely to serve either one in Senegal. While Mommy practiced the placement of the glasses, I folded napkins and drew name cards out in crayon. For Daddy, I wrote *Teddo* in cursive, using my favorite blue crayon, and drew a picture of a black top hat. For Mommy, I wrote *Melanie* in purple and drew a picture of a gold crown. For myself, I wrote *Angela* and drew a picture of a dog. Daddy said that when we moved to Africa, I was definitely getting a dog. "A dog is an all-American pet," he said generously. "And we'll have plenty of room for him to run around outside."

Eventually, we all got hooked. Mommy actually enjoyed reading Emily Post. "Each chapter is like a little story," she said, delighted. She got a kick out of the irony of Post's humor. "You've got to hear this," she'd call out from the kitchen, where she sat, legs propped up across the opposite chair. "All the people are named after their personalities. It's Mrs. Worldly and the Old-worlds, the Eminents, the Onceweres and the Highbrows. Damn, if Emily Post ever visited the Bronx, she would dine with the

Highyellas, the Afrocentrics, the Stillcoloreds, and the Project-bloods."

Mommy not only learned how to set a perfect table, but began to serve dinner by candlelight. Ambiance, she called it. At night, the glow of the candlelight casting shadows over the room, we discussed our plans for Senegal and the many parties we were going to throw in our ambassador's house.

"The first dinner will be in honor of Youssou N'Dour, of course," Daddy said.

"We should invite Stevie Wonder to Senegal," Mommy added, beaming. "I bet he and Youssou will really jam."

Not wanting to be left out, I said, "What about some movie stars? We could invite James Earl Jones and Cicely Tyson."

Daddy loved it. "Great idea, Angela!"

Every night we added to the list of famous people we could entertain in our Senegalese home: Bill Cosby, Harry Belafonte, Sidney Poitier, Isaac Hayes, Gordon Parks, Miles Davis, Carmen de Lavallade, Alvin Ailey. The most exciting part of it all was knowing that when we got to Senegal—we had stopped saying "if" weeks before—all of black America was only a phone call away.

Each day Daddy went to the library to learn more about the foreign service, each night he hammered home his qualifications for serving abroad as if we were the committee that decided. "Shirley Temple was an ambassador to Ghana," he said one evening, shocked beyond belief. "How could they send Miss White America over there and not send me? Ain't gonna happen." We were so taken with the idea that if anyone from the outside asked, "What are you doing next fall?" we would answer with entirely straight faces, "We are going to be ambassadors in West Africa."

In three months' time, the dream evaporated. Daddy stopped

listening to the French tapes, Mommy grew tired of Emily Post. She still set a lovely table and every once in a while we ate by candlelight. The Senegal dream was over, but I never forgot any of it. Nothing but playacting with Daddy off on a tangent, me and Mommy part of the show. But so much of it was real: the sweetness of sitting together as a family for dinner every night, Mommy chuckling to herself as she thumbed through Emily Post, Daddy draped in his daishiki, swaying to the rhythms of the Senegalese pop music, *mbalax*. Even now, when I think of Senegal, it feels like someplace I've been. A place where my parents were good to each other, kissing and hugging and dreaming. Love in plain view.

♣

A brochure advertising the Evelyn Woods speed-reading course was delivered to our house; it was a silvery slip of bait being lowered on fishing wire into Daddy's mouth. From the first enticing lines, Daddy was reeled in. "'Reading Dynamics is a discovery, not an invention,'" my father read theatrically from the course's brochure. "'People have been reading rapidly for centuries. Nineteenth-century economist John Stuart Mill complained he couldn't turn pages as fast as he could read them. Author H. L. Mencken could read a two-hundred-fifty-page book in an hour. U.S. President Theodore Roosevelt read two to three books a day while in office.'" My father's face broke into a wide smile at the mention of President Roosevelt's name. "'To evaluate the course for yourself, we invite you to attend a free Reading Dynamics lesson,'" he continued. He dragged out the words as he read them, so it sounded like "*Read-ing Dy-namics less-on!*" "'At this *one* free lesson, you could increase your reading speed by up to 100 percent.'"

"This is for me!" my father bellowed across the breakfast table. I shoved aside the box of Frosted Flakes so I could see him clearly.

"Is it expensive?" I asked. The refrigerator was empty again and my father did not rush to restock. A sure sign that money was tight.

"And your knowledge shall be your wealth, Jesus said!" my father hollered, now impersonating a Southern preacher. "Not every man has to go to college to be a scholar," he continued. "Look at Gandhi."

"I think Gandhi went to college, Daddy."

"Look at our own prince of peace, Martin Luther King Jr.!"

"Now, you know MLK went to college, Daddy."

"Look at Malcolm X!"

I nodded and continued eating. When we were flush and Daddy flashed dollars like rabbits out of his hat, I threw the soggy cereal away. But the box was light and Daddy seemed broke so I ate more quickly.

"What folks in the ghetto don't understand is that we don't need the *white* man's money and we don't need the *white* man's weapons to win the revolution!" Daddy bellowed with conviction. "They are giving away what we need down at the public library. Nobody's locking up books!"

"I see what you mean, Daddy," I said absently. But what I was thinking was I could care less about the white man or the black man's revolution. I stuck my hand into the cereal box to search for the prize at the bottom. They were giving away Super Friends figures and I already had Zan, one of the Wonder Twins. I was hoping to get Jayna.

"I hate when you do that," Daddy said suddenly, taking the box away from me before I could get the prize. He picked up the Evelyn Woods ad and waved it in my face.

"I'm telling you about the future, about how to improve your mind, and you're reading the back of a cereal box! Come on, Angela. Pay attention. What you need to do, what we all need to do, is read more books," he said. Then he stuck his hand in the cereal box and dug out my prize. Without even looking at it, he pocketed it and walked away.

A week later, the refrigerator was full. There was a new box of Frosted Flakes in the pantry and Daddy coughed up the prize: a Green Lantern that I didn't even want. He was also enrolled in Evelyn Woods. On Tuesday nights, he made a big show of leaving the house at 6 p.m. sharp. Each evening, he dressed in a dark-colored suit, crisp white shirt, and tie. He carried a briefcase that I hadn't seen before. Every week, he packed a book into his case. *The Hierarchy of Heaven and Earth.* Then *Red Land, Black Land: Daily Life in Ancient Egypt.* I couldn't see how he could have gone to class and finished a book in the four hours that he was gone each evening. But it didn't matter.

Five weeks after he started Evelyn Woods, my father was done. I did not need him to tell me this, I just knew because he came home one evening, humming the tune to the Negro National Anthem.

By the time he'd reached the bedroom where I was watching TV, he shifted from humming into full-throttle gospel singing. "Let our rejoicing *r-i-i-i-i-s-e!*" he called out, his warbling not unpleasant. "Up to the listening skies. Let it ring out until victory . . ."

"Lift Every Voice and Sing" was my father's personal battle cry. He sang it in celebration when he was happy; moaned it, like Paul Robeson, in sorrow. When he was angry, the Negro National Anthem calmed him down. When he needed courage, he sang it in fits and starts like the little engine that could, chugging his way uphill. I suspected, though I couldn't prove it, that those first few nights after Mommy left, when I thought I heard my father quietly sobbing through the bedroom wall, the anthem would finally fill his mind and lull him to sleep.

The singing that Tuesday night sounded like a victory march.

"Good class?" I asked, turning Johnny Carson down low.

"My *last* class!" my father said, tossing his suit jacket on the back of a chair.

"The program is only five classes?"

"I only *needed* five classes!" my father said. "Now turn that mess off. We're going to read for an hour before you go to bed."

I looked at the alarm clock on the night table: 11:35.

"Isn't it past my bedtime?" I asked.

"No such thing as bedtime when it comes to combating the ignorance that has been a shackle on our race!" my father preached, a grin on his face. "You know they'd kill a slave for being able to read."

"I know, Daddy," I said, rolling my eyes.

"Well then. Act like you know; go get a book."

I went to the living room and pulled a book out of my knapsack. I returned and crawled into bed next to my father. His book of the day was *Go Tell It on the Mountain*, and he turned to what was clearly the first page. I smirked and opened my book to where I'd left off.

"What are you reading?" my father asked, glancing over at the hardcover in my hand.

"Nancy Drew. *Password to Larkspur Lane*."

"Hmmm," my father muttered, eyeing the blond girl on the cover. "They don't have any black-girl detective stories?"

"I don't think so," I answered, tired and embarrassed that my father made everything, even Nancy Drew, into a comment about race.

"Think so? You better know so. Tomorrow at school, you ask the librarian and find out for sure."

"Okay, Daddy," I answered wearily, intending to ask the librarian, a perfectly nice white lady, no such thing.

I turned to watch my father read. At first, it seemed like he'd developed some sort of weird tic. Every few seconds, his head jumped a little and his chin jutted forward. The slightest of motions, but definitely noticeable. Then I realized that the motion was happening at the end of every line of text, like my daddy's head was a little typewriter bell. He read, read, read, then *brrring!* Read, read, read, then *brrring!* I wondered if that Evelyn Woods woman walked up and down the rows of students, hitting them on the side of their heads with a ruler, forcing them to quickly jump to the next line. The image made me smile, but I didn't let loose a peep, not even a giggle.

♣

The next day when I came home from school, Daddy was typewriter-belling his way through Nancy Drew.

"You finished the Baldwin?" I asked.

"This morning," he said distractedly. He was halfway through the mystery and I could tell he was anxious to know who done it. I didn't ask him why he was reading a book about a white teenager. I just went to the refrigerator and opened a can of Coke.

"This is pretty good," Daddy said, sliding an open box of Oreos toward me. "This girl's no fool. How many books in the series?"

I took the book from him and opened the cover, counted the titles listed inside, and said, "Eighty-six."

"How long will it take you to read them all?"

"Probably a year, Daddy."

"I bet you can do it in six months," he said, extending his own braggadocio to me and my abilities.

"What will you give me for reading so fast?" I asked coyly, sticking out my bony hip and resting my hand there.

"Pride in yourself as a black woman and a reason to hold your head up high!" Daddy declared cheerfully.

"Dream on," I muttered under my breath.

"A place at the front line of the revolution and a stake in a brighter tomorrow!" Daddy continued, as if addressing a pep rally.

I stared him gamely in the eyes, the way Uncle Roger told me he stared down the blackjack fanatics in Atlantic City.

"A dollar a book."

"That's eighty-six dollars."

"I'll save it for college," I said diplomatically.

"I didn't go to college," Daddy said. "I'm telling you, if you read enough, you won't have to go either. That's what I'm trying to *teach* you."

"Fine, then," I said. "I'll save it for Evelyn Woods."

"Very funny."

"Fifty cents a book."

"A quarter."

"You've got a deal," I said, extending my hand to his. I knew my father was not going to pay me. But I didn't care. I'd learned from him and Uncle Roger that hustling was half the fun.

Predictably, he reached behind my ear and pulled out a quarter.

"Cute trick, kid," I said, mimicking his spiel whenever some bar mitzvah boy thought he was Harry Blackstone. "Where'd you learn that? Summer camp?"

"Always the cynic," my father sighed. "You didn't even look at it."

I palmed the coin, then turned it over. A brand-new Susan B. Anthony dollar. I could buy a whole lot of candy at the penny store with this bad boy.

My father stood up and grinned. "The candy store is calling you. I can see it in your eyes. Let's go."

♣

Inside the store, my father walked right over to the display of Reggie Bars. He paused before it, as he always did, as if he was standing before an altar. It didn't matter that, just a few months before, fans at Yankee Stadium were given free Reggie Bars as a promotional gift and instead threw the orange-wrapped chocolate onto the field, booing the arrogant Jackson and causing a game delay. Daddy didn't care. Reggie Jackson was his man. Mr. October could do no wrong in his eyes.

"Steinbrenner's a racist," Daddy growled at the TV. "Billy Martin's a punk." My father was not much of a sports fan, but then again what he loved about Reggie Jackson had very little to do with baseball. What Daddy liked was Jackson's swagger. He loved to watch Jackson grandstand at a press conference. Days after Jackson was quoted as saying he was the best thing going for the Yankees, Daddy was still walking around mimicking him. "I'm the straw that stirs the drink," Daddy said playfully. "It all comes from me. I've got to keep it going." Once Reggie Jackson joined the Yanks, for Daddy, baseball was the all-African-American pastime. "Look at that bat," Daddy said, collapsing into giggles. "Brother got himself a *black* bat. Calls it the 'Dues Collector.' Reggie's gone Mandingo on those fools and none of those Yankee pinstripes can handle it. Not Munson, not Sparky Lyle, not Lou Pinella. Not one of them can handle a strong black man whose talent is so unstoppable."

Mommy had been spectacularly unimpressed with Reggie Jackson. "Why's he always in the paper with some white woman?" she'd ask my father. "If he's the symbol of black pride you say he is, why can't he romance a sister?" My father just rolled his eyes. "Petty jealousy," he said. "You know how those gossip columnists are. They probably don't take any pictures when he's with black women. Wouldn't be front-page news, then." Mommy didn't respond, but I noted her suspicion and kept a little of it for myself.

The spring after Mommy left, my father and I began to watch baseball together. My father couldn't explain the plays very well, but he saw a morality lesson in every swing Jackson took. One day my father turned to me and spoke in a voice that was filled with neither braggadocio nor black pride. He said softly, "It makes me want to cry the way they treat that black man on that team. They don't give him the respect they gave Babe Ruth or Joe DiMaggio or Mickey Mantle. Reggie Jackson hit his fiftieth home run in the last two months of the season and he still can't catch a break. To them, he's just a nigger who can hit a ball. But watch him, Angela. He's a great man."

I thought about what Mommy said about Reggie Jackson and his passion for white women and about the pictures I saw on TV of Jackson's ninety-thousand-dollar Rolls-Royce. Daddy took me to the candy store to buy a Reggie Bar, but I didn't want to. Reggie Jackson was not going to starve if I didn't spend my one silver dollar on his stupid old candy bar. I didn't even collect the baseball cards that came inside.

"You know Reggie Bars don't uplift the people," I said, challenging his quiet reverie. "They just make a rich guy richer. He's an athlete, not a revolutionary."

My father looked stricken. "You don't know what Reggie Jackson might be doing for the people. A lot of famous black people can't advertise their radical views, but they write the checks. Who do you think financed the Black Panthers? Who do you think paid for the breakfast program?"

I didn't say anything as I turned to examine my options. The silver dollar in my pocket could buy four of my favorite Whatchamacallits or I could make the money last longer by spending just a quarter on two blow pops and five pieces of penny candy.

"Besides," my father said, spinning my shoulders so that I faced him and looking at me plaintively, "any black man who crosses the color line, any man who can have whites in the stands cheering on their feet as if they'd never heard or thought the word nigger—any man who can do that deserves our support."

My father picked up a Reggie Bar then walked to the counter to pay for it. Whenever my father wanted to purchase something, he never let his arms drop to his side. He held the object up at eye level, like a basketball he was aiming to shoot. My father held the Reggie Bar up to the shopkeeper, then still holding it high, he reached into his pocket and slapped a quarter on the counter.

As much as my father talked about black pride and black power, there was a dance he did around white people. Maybe he found the dance degrading. Maybe he found it infuriating. But it had the opposite effect on me. I watched my father's careful gestures in the white world and I saw all the places where he was vulnerable and all the ways he tried to protect himself against forces he could not control. At these times, he was easy to admire and easy to love. I picked up a Reggie Bar, paid for it, and followed my dad out of the store.

The Apple, the Tree, and All

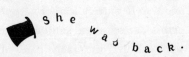 She was back.

I could smell her in the house before I actually saw her. I woke that night to the same divine mixture of Jean Naté, Avon Skin So Soft, and TCB hair grease. I looked at the Mickey Mouse clock by my bed, the bright numbers that glowed in the dark: almost 3 a.m. I wondered when Mommy's flight had come in. How long did it take to fly from California to New York? I hadn't heard a knock at the front door or the doorbell but, of course, she did not ring the bell. My father must have gone out and picked her up or sent her keys. I could hear Mommy and Daddy in the kitchen, the low rumbling of revved-up conversation, the kind of laughter that only followed jokes I could not get. I wanted to jump out of bed and run to her, wrap my arms around her and welcome her home, but I resisted. It had been five months since Mommy was gone and I wanted her to discover me, like Sleeping Beauty, in my bed. I rubbed a little spit on my finger and wiped the sides of my mouth. I smoothed out my ponytail puffs and tried to arrange them artfully on my pillow, where I rested my head ever so delicately. I closed my eyes and smiled without showing any teeth and imagined that I was in the middle of the sweetest dream. I waited for the scent to grow stronger and told myself that not until I felt Mommy's lips on my cheek would I open my eyes. I lay this way, poised for my fairy-tale ending, for probably all of five minutes before the hour and my own exhaustion overtook me and I fell back asleep.

In the morning, I shook the pretense, galloping to the kitchen where my father sat, sipping his morning coffee, with a woman who was not my mother. She was about Mommy's height, with the same straight shoulder-length hair. She was wearing a boatneck red-and-yellow T-shirt and a pair of red flared pants. Her platform shoes were buttery leather with red-and-yellow butterflies darting across her toes. She smiled at me broadly and opened both arms wide. "Don't just stand there, Miss Angela," she said. "Give me some sugar."

I didn't move until my father jerked his head toward the stranger with a look that said I better get to stepping or I'd pay for it later. After the Danita episode, I was too scared to ask who this woman might be. Nobody explained.

"I'm fixing your father some breakfast," the woman said, fussing with the pots underneath the sink as if she knew our kitchen inside and out. "I wanted to have breakfast ready for when you woke up, but I've been cleaning for an hour. This place was a mess. Some of the things in the fridge were starting to look like a science experiment."

She poured a cup of orange juice in front of me. "You like juice, right? It's going to take me a minute to make you some hot cocoa."

I gulped the juice down.

The lady smiled at me, "You're welcome."

Our kitchen never felt smaller. I became intensely interested in the sunflowers on the wallpaper. I knew they were sunflowers because of their shape, but the wallpaper was so old that the petals were a kind of muddy orange and the parts that used to be white were a kind of tan. "Thank you for the juice," I said to the wall.

"So, Angela, I'm making pancakes, bacon, and scrambled eggs. How does that sound to you?"

Was this woman a maid or a cook? Did my father hit the magician's jackpot? Were we moving on up to a deluxe apartment on the East Side? I kept my eyes trained on the sunflowers, trying to read them like tea leaves for some answers.

"Angela, please, stop acting like you lost the sense that God gave you," my father said. "Speak up, black woman!"

I kept up my staring, at the wall when she was looking at me, at the woman when she wasn't.

"It's okay, Teddo," the woman said. Then she kissed me on the forehead.

She could have been a chef, though, the way she cooked. There were blueberries in the pancakes; I'd never seen anything so fancy. In my unabashed staring, I'd seen her dip the bacon in maple syrup before she fried it. The best bacon I'd ever tasted. Little green things were suspended in the eggs. "Chives," she said when she saw me examining my fork for the secret of delicious.

My father was slurping down the eggs like he had teeth in the back of his throat. "They're spicy, too," he said, his mouth full.

"A little bit of Tabasco," she said, winking at my father.

She seduced me with food and I felt guilty. The soft spicy taste of eggs, the syrupy bacon. I didn't exactly want her to stay, but how could I wish for her to leave without knowing who she was? I turned to eye the stove, to see if the black cast-iron skillet was empty, and she jumped to her feet.

"Plenty more where that came from," she said, heaping more food on my plate. I ate in silence while the woman and my father made small talk about music, their favorite records, and which clubs were still hot. But the more I listened to them talk, the more it became clear that they'd known each other for a long time.

"You ever see Doug Parker?"

"You mean little Dougie Parker from 118th Street?"

My dad smiled. "When he was your man, you didn't let anyone call him little or Dougie."

She slammed her hand on our kitchen table and I saw that her fingernails were bright pink. I was pretty sure that neither her red lipstick or her pink nail polish came from the Revlon Polished Amber collection Mommy used to wear.

"Teddo, now, please," she said. "I didn't come all the way from Chicago for you to start digging bones out of my closet."

I put my fork down. "You're from Chicago?"

My father rolled his eyes. "Come on, Angela. I don't know why you're walking around here like the Bride of Frankenstein. You know your Aunt Mona is from Chicago."

I looked at the woman sitting next to me—the way she was dressed in Saturday night clothes on a Sunday morning—and my breath started to get heavy. I had not seen Mommy in her, yet once my father said it I couldn't stop. Like a kaleidoscope, Mommy's face spun in front of me: sixteen versions of her smile swirling like a tunnel of colored glass, sixteen pairs of her eyes sparkling like a handful of confetti thrown in the air. I was prepared for this woman, this stranger, to be a girlfriend, a real contender with her nice clothes, sweet smile, all that food, and the butterflies dancing across her shoes. But for her to be Mommy's sister, to be Mommy's anything, was so cruel.

I was little when my Aunt Mona moved to Chicago. Mommy told me that I'd known her as a toddler, but I didn't remember. Mommy didn't have one single picture of Aunt Mona as a grown-up, just faded portraits of them at five and eight, and twelve and fifteen dressed like twins. The way Mommy described her older sister made me imagine that Mona was some cross between Aunt Esther from *Sanford and Son* and sassy-mouthed Willona from *Good Times*. I was not expecting a pretty young woman who could have passed for Mommy if you only met Mommy once at a party or briefly on the street.

I asked my father if I could be excused and the minute I said it, I was reminded of the schoolyard taunt "Ain't no excuse for the kind of ugly you got." But my father waved me away with the exasperated look that I'd seen Russian coaches on TV give their girl gymnasts after a poor performance.

"You must be very tired," Aunt Mona said, caressing my face with her bubble gum fingers.

I nodded and went back to bed, grateful that no one seemed to mind that I had just gotten up.

♥

In my bed, with the door closed and the curtains drawn, the room was as quiet as a hospital. I tried to imagine the walls without all the pictures taped to them, walls as white as a sick bay. Mommy was not there to help me decorate this room, but I'd carefully cut out pictures from *Essence* and *Right On!* magazines to re-create the room Mommy helped me decorate before she left. There was a pinup of Michael Jackson and one of Stacy Lattisaw. I found the same ad in *Essence* that Mommy loved, the one of opera singer Jessye Norman swathed in a Blackglama mink coat. "What becomes a legend most?" Mommy purred, pretending that her cotton coat was a fur draped across her shoulders. "Blackglama!"

I wanted to be sick. I wanted to throw up the pancakes, the bacon, the blueberries, the eggs, the chives—all that food, disloyalty, stupidity. I wanted to throw up the night before, when I mistook the smell of my aunt for the smell of Mommy and I lay in the dark, primping and waiting for the good-night kiss that would make my life normal again. It was Mona I heard in the night, not Melanie. But my stomach didn't care. It did not let me be sick no matter how far I pressed my fingers down the back of my throat. I'd seen a girl do the very same thing to stay slim on an afterschool special. It wasn't working for me. More proof that my father was right. The things that white kids can do on TV never work for black kids in real life.

Just outside the door I heard footsteps, heavy trying to be light, like my father tiptoeing when he got in late from a show. I heard water, the sink, dishes and pots being scrubbed. Then music. Smokey Robinson singing, "Why do you want to get on my bad side?" I crawled deeper under the covers and wished it all away.

♥

By dinnertime, I was too hungry to continue my sleep-in. I went to the bathroom, brushed my teeth, and changed out of my pajamas into what Mommy called home clothes. Home clothes were school clothes that were too ratty to wear out. Every September, Mommy went through my closet and pulled out a few things that no longer made the grade: a sweater whose pills defied repair, pants so worn that the butt was shiny. Then she'd fold them neatly and put them in the bottom drawer of my white wood dresser. "Home clothes!" she'd say cheerily, like we'd just discovered something unexpected, like a dollar in the pocket of a coat you haven't worn since winter or an extra slice of pie, hidden at the back of the fridge.

I leaned against the dresser for a moment, realizing for the first time that in real life a person's gifts do not disappear when they do. In "Cinderella," at midnight, everything goes—the fairy god-mother, the dress, the horses, the carriage. But when Mommy left, every material thing that I associated with her stayed behind—her records, her straightening comb, most of her clothes, this dresser. The dresser was white with gold ribbons painted on each drawer. There was a big mirror with wavy edges and more gold ribbons painted as a kind of trim.

Mommy paid down for nearly two years to buy me that dresser on layaway at Levine's Furniture on Flatbush. The month before she left, she'd taken me there on a Saturday. Two buses and a train from the Bronx. She wanted me to see the matching canopy bed she'd been paying down on. After she left, I wondered what happened to my bed and how much money Mommy had already put down. But I did not want to anger my father by asking. Maybe a little part of me thought that when Mommy came home, she would want to get the bed herself.

♥

For two weeks, my Aunt Mona was like this strange but amiable angel. She fell into our lives and kept the apartment spotless. My father said she was saving him a small fortune by hand washing and ironing his shirts. She made me lunch every day, never anything as simple as peanut butter and jelly. Each time she concocted something that made half the lunchroom turn and stare when I unwrapped it, like a Cuban pressed sandwich with ham and manchego cheese or pulled pork on a roll, with the barbecue sauce dripping down the side. She was there when I came home from school and was awake in the morning when my father was still sleeping. She slept in the living room, though she kept the sofa spotless; the sheet and blankets were folded neatly on the side by the time I got up. She became the third point of our triangle. She held the household down.

My father stopped letting me go to nightclubs and, more and more, Aunt Mona went with him. When I complained, he pretended that my disco nights were a one-off, instead of a regular thing. "I probably shouldn't have taken you to those clubs in the first place, you know," he said, tucking me in one night before he went out for the evening. "It's just that I'd rather have you with me than hire a babysitter. But you're old enough, aren't you, sweetheart? You can stay home by yourself. It's just for a few hours."

"I'm his bodyguard," Aunt Mona joked. She hovered behind my father, waiting for her turn to kiss me good night. It bugged me a little the way she was constantly hugging and kissing me, but I figured that if I ate the food, I needed to take the kisses.

Aunt Mona was wearing a white silk halter and royal blue genie pants with big gold hoops in her ears. "I'll protect him from treacherous barflies," she said. Her lips were a shiny red and she laughed in a husky, wicked way that made me wonder if there was something she was saying that I wasn't grown-up enough to catch.

One afternoon when Aunt Mona was out grocery shopping, I asked my father how long she was planning to stay.

"I don't know," he said. He sat on the floor of the living room, sorting out decks of cards. Many of our decks were useless but my father never knew which was which. Only a brand-new deck was guaranteed to be trick free. Every couple of weeks, Daddy went through the piles to see if there were any worth saving.

"Why is she here?" I asked.

"I don't know. To help us out, I guess," Daddy said. He held a deck in his hands and four piles in front of him. The longest suit was diamonds. He'd lined them up from the king of diamonds to the three of diamonds.

"Do you think she's heard from Mommy?" I asked, bracing myself against the sofa for the tongue-lashing that was sure to come.

"Honestly, I don't think so," my father said, looking up at me. His eyes were sad.

"Is that because Mommy didn't like her?"

My father turned over the five of hearts and three of spades. "No."

"Did you ask her?" I pushed.

My father's face was tighter than a brand-new deck of cards. "I stopped asking people about your mother months ago, Angela," he said.

I went over to where he sat and I hugged him from behind. "I love you, Daddy," I whispered into his ear.

He turned and gave me his best Teddo, the Amazing Magician, smile. "Pick a card," he said, shuffling the deck in his hand with a tornado-like flourish. "Any card."

♥

A few days later, I came home from school and my father was at the magic shop. My Aunt Mona was making dinner, one of my new favorites: fried chicken and waffles.

I took a seat at the kitchen table to watch her cook. "Aunt Mona, do you have any idea where Mommy is?"

"Well," she said, "you know me and your mother were not very close." The front left burner was on low and Aunt Mona held a raw chicken leg over the flame, burning off any stray hairs that might have been left on the bird.

"It's okay," I said, reaching into the fridge for a pitcher of Kool-Aid. Aunt Mona made the best Kool-Aid; she spiced it up with ginger ale and slices of lemon and orange.

"Why are you asking me about Melanie, pumpkin?" She reached for another chicken leg. "Do you miss her that bad?"

"Yeah," I said, slurping the bottom of the glass with a bendy straw. Aunt Mona brought home a whole box of crazy straws, just for me.

"Aren't you glad I came?" she asked, turning up the flame even higher.

"Yeah, of course."

"Then why are you asking me about your mother?" Her words were rough and scratchy.

"I just miss her, like you said." I knew the minute that the "m" in "miss" hit my tongue I'd start crying. I turned my head to the wall.

Aunt Mona grabbed me with her chicken hand and yanked me over to the stove. The grip on my wrist was cold and clammy.

"All the cooking and cleaning I've been doing and here you go, talking about how you miss your mommy, you miss your mommy."

She took a piece of raw chicken and rubbed it up and down the inside of my left wrist.

"I never met a child so ungrateful!" she said, drawing in her chest as if she was about to brave a very rough storm.

I tried to pull my arm away, thinking that surely the chicken rub had been punishment enough. But she pulled my arm back over the stove and held it in the flame. I screamed, an animal sound that frightened me almost more than the pain.

"Say, 'Thank you, Aunt Mona.'"

I repeated the phrase, pulling my arm away. The inside of my wrist was throbbing, but the cool air felt like heaven. But Aunt Mona wasn't done. She pulled my arm into the flame again.

"Please stay forever, Aunt Mona," she said.

It hurt so bad the second time around that the words sputtered like hot oil through my tears. Please. (Burn.) Stay. (Burn.) Forever. (Burn.)

I grabbed the arm close to me and it stuck to my T-shirt. I yanked it away, but a thin layer of cotton now covered the burn.

"Look what you did, you damn fool," Aunt Mona said.

She reached into the fridge and grabbed a stick of butter. "Put this on it."

"I'm okay," I muttered, stepping backward.

She uncovered the butter stick and said, "Come on now, this will help."

My aunt rubbed the butter on my arm and I could barely stand still, fearful of what she might do next. "This is the story," she said as she massaged the stick across the burn. "You wanted to help me fry up the chicken and you burned your arm. Got it?"

I nodded.

She grabbed my good hand and pulled me close to her. "Don't mess with me, little girl. I can make it so you wish you were never born."

♥

I closed the door to my room and wished for a lock. Every time Mona dropped a piece of chicken in the pan, I flinched at the sizzling sound. The pain of the burn was excruciating. I took the pencils out of my art kit and began to draw another comic. I drew a picture of Storm, Professor Xavier, and me. Then I began to letter my first panel:

♥♥♥

STORM INTRODUCES PROFESSOR XAVIER TO HER
LITTLE SISTER, SUMMER SHOWER.

♥♥♥

It was a good X-Men name, Summer Shower, and I was so excited about it that I decided to write a letter to Stan Lee at Marvel Comics. Maybe Stan Lee would offer me a job. Maybe he had a boarding school for talented kids who drew comic books, just like Professor Xavier's school for exceptional mutants. I heard a knock on my door and jumped to open it. Daddy! The word was out of my mouth before my hand even touched the door knob.

Mona stopped inches from me and smiled. "Come on, sweetie. Dinner is served."

It took Daddy until his second helping of chicken and waffles to notice the burn on my arm.

"Who bit ya?" he asked, reaching out to touch my hand.

I looked down and noticed he was right. The red shiny patch

on my arm looked a lot like a dog bite. I was all ready to give him Mona's story, but she beat me to it.

"This sweet thing was trying to help me out with the cooking. But the only thing she fried was that arm. She'll be okay."

I smiled at my father. I was okay. Mona never touched me again, and I never mentioned Mommy to her again. She still made my lunch though now I ate it like a girl with a gun to her head. I was convinced that she was spitting in it.

♥

One afternoon, nearly a month into Mona's stay, my father was emptying his suit pockets, in anticipation of his weekly trip to the cleaners. My father's pockets were like Russian dolls nestled inside of each other. His pockets had pockets that had pockets. I sat on the edge of his bed and watched him pull out cards, bits of rope, red rubber balls, fake quarters, real quarters, balloons, even tiny, pocket-sized screwdrivers.

"Does Aunt Mona have a boyfriend?" I asked. It seemed to me that a boyfriend might be the only way to get Aunt Mona out of the house without her laying another finger on me.

"She did. In Chicago."

"What about here?"

"I don't know. Roger's kind of sweet on her, but I told him those Lewis women are a handful. The apple, the tree, and all."

"What?"

"She is your mother's sister. That kind of crazy," my father said, "is a family affair."

"Mommy isn't crazy!" I said, jumping to my feet. "She never . . ."

My father draped his jackets and pants across his arm, like they were a linen napkin and he was a waiter in a fine restaurant.

"She never what, sweetheart?" he said, balancing the weight of the clothes and reaching out to grab his wallet off the dresser. "She never left? She not only left her husband, she left her kid. No sane woman pulls a stunt like that."

He kissed me on the forehead. "I'm outta here. Tell Mona to be ready by nine."

I nodded.

"Watch TV in my bedroom if you want, okay?"

♥

I am not sure whether instinct or dumb luck prompted me to search Aunt Mona's suitcase. I knew that if I got caught, Mona's punishment was sure. But I also knew that there was something in that suitcase that I wanted to see. Mona and my father were at Odyssey. My father had a show and they were going out afterward. They rarely returned before 2 a.m. Plenty of time.

I put on a pair of yellow kitchen gloves, not because I honestly believed that Mona checked for fingerprints, but because they somehow seemed an apt reminder of just how much trouble I would get in. I lifted each pile of clothes out carefully: all of Mona's fancy disco clothes, the outfit she was wearing on the first day she showed up, and two white cotton Asian-style jackets with her name stitched in script across the pocket. Some kind of uniform, but I couldn't tell for what. There was an old bulky phone book with lots of scraps of papers, coasters, and matchbooks paper-clipped to the pages. I handled it like a bomb. There was a clip-on laminated ID of Mona in a white uniform jacket. It said: KITCHEN STAFF, DRAKE HOTEL, CHICAGO, and there was the hotel's fancy logo. I wondered what she did in the kitchen. Was she a chef? Did she wash dishes and learn how to cook by watching? I knew I'd never ask her.

Then I found it. An eight-by-ten-inch picture of Mommy, kind of like my father's magician head shot, but different. There was no resume with a phone number and address on the back. That was the first thing I looked for. Simply a photo. Four smaller photos, actually, all printed on one page. Each photograph showed Mommy dressed up a different way. In the upper left-hand corner, she was dressed in a slinky V-neck dress with a long row of pearls slung around her neck. Her hair was blown out and wavy; she smiled seductively at the camera. She looked glamorous and rich. Really rich. There was a gigantic diamond ring on her right hand; I could see it because she held the pearls slightly forward with the same hand.

In the upper right-hand photograph, she was dressed in a preppy white polo shirt and she held a tennis racket with both hands, like she was ready to give it a powerful swing. Her hair was in a ponytail and she was wearing a white terry visor. Her makeup was subtler in this photograph, just a little blush on her cheeks and her lips were shiny.

In the bottom left-hand photograph, she was dressed like an executive. She was wearing a plaid suit jacket with a gold brooch on one lapel. Underneath the jacket, she was wearing a white silk blouse with a floppy tie. Her hair was pulled back in a bun and she wore a pair of tortoiseshell glasses. She was holding a manila folder in one hand, and in the other, a fancy pen.

The final photograph was the hardest to take. I kept trying to concentrate on the other images, but this was the one that kept drawing me back. Mommy was wearing a paisley-print peasant blouse. Her hair fell in loose ringlets around her shoulders, a style I'd never seen her wear in real life. She was wearing what looked like no makeup at all, and she was staring into the eyes of a baby that she cradled lovingly in her arms. I counted backward and I knew that in the six months she'd been gone, she could not have had a baby, but I felt replaced nonetheless. I could not tell if the baby was a boy or a girl, but he or she was brown and beautiful, with curly black hair that barely covered its little baby head.

Seeing that baby made me steal the photograph. I told myself that Mona must have stolen the photograph from someone. I was sure Mommy did not send it to her. But even after justifying the morality, I needed a plan: what was I going to do when Mona figured out that the photo was gone? She was going to hurt me. Having the photograph was worth it.

I laid the photograph to the side and carefully repacked Mona's suitcase. Then I walked around the apartment trying to decide where to hide it. In my room, good as gone. It was a miracle that neither my father nor Mona found the brown silk scarf with the straightening comb, toothbrush, the collected scraps of my mother's handwriting, and my parents' wedding photo wrapped inside. I thought of hiding the photo in my father's room, but the chances of him finding it seemed too great. Even the back of his closet, with its empty shoeboxes and the old files of leaflets and reports from what my father called his "subversive era," felt unsafe.

Then I hit on the perfect place: my parents' record collection. The photo could slip right inside between the white sheath that held the record and the actual dust jacket. The trick was finding the right album. It must be something that neither my father nor Mona might get a hankering to play in the near future. All the disco albums were out. So were Marvin Gaye, Marlena Shaw, Ashford and Simpson, and Patti LaBelle. I thumbed through the piles of records nervously. It was nearly midnight and my father's show was probably finished. If Mona wasn't feeling well or my father changed his mind about going out, then they could be home in as soon as half an hour. An older album would be good. I reached for Nat King Cole, but my father sometimes got nostalgic and wanted to hear old King Cole. The Impressions were chancy for the same reason. Then I saw it, an old Mahalia Jackson album Mommy loved. I slipped the photo in and went to bed, confident that no one in our house was going to be playing a gospel album anytime soon.

A few hours later, I heard Mona and my father come in. Their voices were garbled from the living room, but soon, I could hear Teddy Pendergrass on the turntable. Something was strange. My father never played music when he came in. Too late. It was at least two o'clock in the morning, if not three or four. I wanted to get up and sneak a peek, but I was too afraid of Mona's eagle eye catching me. I stood up and pressed my ear to the door.

I thought I heard kissing sounds and then they stopped. Then I heard the sounds again. I heard my father whisper, "We shouldn't." Then I heard Mona say, "Come on, Teddo, what does Melanie got that I don't have?" Pretty soon, I was sure that what I heard was more than kissing. The sound was the wet, naked kind I hadn't heard in the house since before Mommy left. I went back to my bed and covered my head with my pillow, humming to myself so I wouldn't have to hear them panting. I counted to one hundred and then one hundred again. I lifted the pillow and heard my father walk from the living room to the bathroom. Then I heard him slam the door and the shower was turned on, full blast. A few minutes later, the shower was turned off. My father's bedroom door opened and closed.

♥

Early the next morning, I was awakened by the sound of screaming.

"Fuck you, Teddo," my Aunt Mona yelled.

"I'd like you to leave," my father said back, using his supercalm voice.

"Make me go, you fucking punk," she screamed back.

"Don't make me call the police, Mona," my father said, raising his voice now.

I heard the phone being thumped upon the table once, twice, then again. "Call them, you bitch-ass nigger. Tell them about how you fucked me last night and now you're sorry."

"Come on, Mona," my father said, dropping his voice as if this made hers less audible. "Angela is still sleeping."

"Wake the little bitch up!" Mona screamed. "Wake up, you little bastard bitch! Let me tell you all about your mommy the ho and your daddy the limp-dick motherfucker."

My father was silent. I never learned what he did in that moment. But the next thing I heard was Mona screaming, "No, you didn't!"

Then she left, slamming the door behind her.

♥

I jumped back into bed and lay as still as I could until I heard my father knock on my door.

"You sleeping?" he asked.

I shook my head. "No."

"How much did you hear?"

I shrugged. "Is she gone?"

My father said, "Yes."

"Are you sure?" I asked, trying hard to contain my joy.

"We won't starve," he said with a grin, misinterpreting my tentativeness for sadness.

"You'll miss those chicken and waffles," I said.

"Not like I miss your mother," he said, rubbing my cheek. "I really miss your mother."

I wanted to say something about how I missed her, too; to show him the photograph I'd lifted from Mona's bag; to explain how I actually got the burn on my arm. But I didn't.

How Misguided My Affections

My Father

had a sweet ride. Twenty years old, but still a beauty. A bronze-colored Mercedes with a cream leather interior. All the guys in the neighborhood called it a white man's car. They'd say if my father wanted something styling, he should get himself a Cadillac. This offended my father to no end.

"A pimpmobile?" he asked, incredulous. "You've got to be kidding. Brothers want to get up in the world, they've got to modify their tastes."

I was outside waiting for Daddy to take me to the Jamaican beef patty shop for lunch but Daddy wasn't hungry, he was too busy shining his car and talking trash to Uncle Roger and Sammy. Daddy was wearing a pair of burgundy polyester pants that flared ever so slightly beneath his knees, a white shirt with thin burgundy-and-green stripes. It was an especially warm May day, and as a concession to the heat Daddy wore a pair of brown leather sandals. He never wore jeans or sneakers, not even to wash the car.

"Nice toes," Uncle Roger said when he arrived, looking Baraka fierce in a navy blue tunic top and a strand of heavy-looking onyx beads.

"Teddo done got himself some man sandals," Sammy snickered, jumping out of a gypsy cab in front of our house.

"Where were you last night?" Daddy asked Roger. "You missed my show."

"I was at the Kool Jazz festival," Uncle Roger said, his voice all grits and greens. "You know me. I'm Miles without a trumpet. I needed to check those brothers out."

"Who was there?" Sammy asked.

"Smokey was there," Roger said, shooting Sammy a watch-your-mouth glance. Roger was serious about jazz music and Sammy was serious about nothing.

"They had to have Smokey," Daddy said, nodding approvingly. "Did he sing that new single?"

Roger smiled broadly. "'Why Do You Wanna See My Bad Side'? Smokey tore that joint up!"

"Who else was there?" Sammy asked.

"The Staple Singers."

"I know a place, ain't nobody crying . . ." Sammy began to sing, launching into the Staple Singers' most famous song.

"Who else?" Daddy asked, shooting Sammy a look.

"Natalie Cole."

"I know a place . . ." Sammy began, once again.

Roger looked fed up. "Now you know that's not a Natalie Cole song."

"You didn't let me finish," Sammy said. "I know a place . . ." He paused for dramatic effect and whispered, "It's called my bedroom . . . Ain't no women crying."

Daddy just grinned. "Yeah, right. Ain't no smiling faces up in there either."

"Sho you're right," Roger said, reaching out to give Daddy five.

Sammy wasn't going to take the dozens lying down. "As if those man sandals are going to get you any ladies, Teddo."

Daddy just shrugged them off. "Men in Italy wear them all the time," he said. "Bet you fools never even heard of Giorgio Armani."

Uncle Roger just laughed out loud. "Well, you better get yourself over to Italy and start hanging with Mr. Armani. 'Cause here in New York, you look like John Lennon's colored homie."

"Damn straight," Sammy said. "They ought to sell those shoes with a plane ticket." He then put on a voice, even more feminine than his own, "Nice taking your money, Mr. Brown. Have a nice flight."

Daddy tried to change the subject. "Did you know that ninety-two percent of black folks voted for Carter in 1976?"

"And I'll vote for him again," said Uncle Roger.

"If we endorse Carter, or Ted Kennedy for that matter, what kind of bargaining power will we have?" Daddy asked. All of a sudden, he was serious as a heart attack.

Sammy just stood there, lamping. "What you know about bargaining, Teddo? Did you bargain your way out of hell by agreeing to wear those shoes?"

Roger pointed in Sammy's direction with all the flourish of a ref giving the other team the ball.

"You fellas don't know nothing about style. Matter of fact, when I start making some serious cash," Daddy said, bent on one knee, diligently polishing the silvery hubcaps, "I'm going to get me an Aston Martin."

"A what?" Roger asked.

"Aston Martin. It's a British sports car," Daddy said. "Kind of car that James Bond drives. I'm gonna get me one of those cars. Forget about being Super Fly. I'm gonna be a Super Spy."

"You look more like a Shoe Fly to me, Sandal Man," Sammy cracked. All the guys started laughing then; Daddy was the loudest of them all.

"You one crazy Negro, Teddo," Uncle Roger said. The way he said it, it was as if Daddy wasn't crazy at all, but imaginative and more than a little brave. That's what I thought anyway.

Sammy pouted; he hated when my father and Uncle Roger didn't pay him any attention. Whenever he sensed he was boring them, he brought up girls. "I know you fellas don't go for no snowflakes," Sammy said, sliding around Daddy's car like he was a snake, off to take Eve to the prom. "But did y'all catch the Dinah Shore show last night? That white woman is *hot*."

Daddy flicked a wet rag at Sammy and he jumped back, barely missing the soaking. "Now you know that Dinah Shore is old," Daddy said. "Too old."

Sammy shrugged. "Good enough for Burt Reynolds. She's good enough for me." He licked his lips then made the same exact finger-in-the-hole hand motion that the boys at my school did whenever they started talking about doing the nasty. "That old white lady must have some kind of *Kama Sutra* secret."

No one seemed to mind that I was present. When my mother was around, my father's friends kept the conversation clean, even when she was at work and couldn't possibly hear a word that they said. Back then, they stopped right before the good part, mumbling tired clichés about little pitchers and big ears. Now that Mommy had been gone for half a year, Daddy's buddies no longer minded their manners and I'd overheard plenty.

Uncle Roger cocked one eyebrow. "'Course she's got sex appeal, fool. Everybody know that Dinah Shore's got a little coffee in her milk."

My father stood up from where he was kneeling, lovingly washing the silver hubcaps of his car. "Tell the truth, now? Old Dinah is passing?"

Uncle Roger nodded. "That woman is colored! My grandmother used to call her Pinky."

Sammy burst out laughing. "Pinky! Now that's funny. Sign me up then! I'm *all* about the café au lait."

♠

I did not know how much money Daddy really made. He drove that old Mercedes, dressed every day in tailored suits and designer shoes that he went all the way to Manhattan to buy. Daddy dressed nicer than Uncle Roger or Sammy. Yet sometimes there was hardly any food in the house, and Uncle Roger would show up with an armful of groceries, like it was nothing, he was just stopping by.

One afternoon, we were driving to Long Island for one of Daddy's shows. We did not have breakfast and Daddy said we'd eat after the performance.

I just straight out asked him. "Daddy, are we broke?"

I thought the question irked him, but he just flipped it right back to me.

"What do you think? Does a man in a nice suit like this look poor to you?"

I shook my head no.

"How about this car? Nice car, huh? What kind of car is this?"

I took a deep breath then, preparing myself for the litany of questions that I'd heard so many times before.

"Mercedes."

"Where are Mercedeses from?"

"Germany," I answered softly.

"Meaning what?"

"That this is a foreign import car."

"Which are more expensive than?"

"Domestic cars like Fords," I answered, thumbing the lock on the passenger door as if escape was even possible. I got on Daddy's nerves and now he meant to school me. It was question after question, the whole ride down.

"How about these seats?" he asked, with an aggravated sideways glare. He ran his hand over my headrest and I flinched slightly. Daddy almost never hit me, but that didn't mean he didn't know how to scare the bejesus out of me.

"Are these plastic like in Roger's car?"

"No, Daddy."

"Do they squeak when you sit in them—even in the heat?"

"No, Daddy."

"What are they made of?"

"Leather," I said, reaching to turn up the car radio. Chaka Khan was singing "Tell Me Something Good" and I was wishing I'd never opened my fat trap.

"And leather is . . ." Daddy continued, turning the music back down.

I tried to ignore him, gazing intently at the row of pines that dotted the Long Island Expressway.

"Did you hear me?" my father asked, placing his hand on my shoulder a little too roughly. I knew my father so well and still I broke the rules. Talking back was okay. Even the occasional cuss word was acceptable, especially now that Mommy wasn't around to get offended. But I ignored him at my peril. My father needed an audience at all times.

"Leather is expensive, Daddy," I answered obediently.

"So the answer to your question is . . ."

"What question?"

"The question about whether or not I am a man who can provide for my family. The question that implied that I don't have a pot to piss in or a window to throw it out of is what . . ."

"We are not broke," I answered, while silently I prayed for God to Krazy Glue my lips together. Forever and ever. Amen.

♠

I was walking home from school one afternoon, when a deep voice called out to me.

"Hey, pretty."

I did not turn to look, then the voice spoke again.

"I said hey, pretty."

He was one of the mechanics in the gas station that I passed every day. He was maybe thirty years old, with skin the color of cinnamon and what the girls at school called "pretty eyes." I couldn't tell what color they were from where I stood—which was close, but within running distance. He wore a dirty pair of army-green overalls. There was more oil in his voice than there was on his pants.

"I don't talk to strangers," I said in a haughty voice and turned on my heels.

"I'm not a stranger!" the man said, indignant. "I'm Edward, a friend of your father's. Don't you remember me?"

I turned around slowly, trying to remember. My father knew so many people.

I took a few steps toward the mechanic, trying to place his face. Cranked high above the ground, sick cars hung suspended while the mechanics performed their greasy surgery. I could smell the sweet, burning smell of ganja, and on the oversized tape deck Marvin Gaye was asking, "What's happening brother?" No one in the garage seemed to pay me or my new friend any mind.

"You work on my daddy's car?" I asked.

"You bet I do," he said, grinning.

"The Mercedes?" I blurted out as if Daddy owned more than one car.

"One and the same," the mechanic said. "Now, don't I do a nice job?"

I nodded.

"He sure loves that car," he continued. "It's a pretty ride. Not as pretty as you."

I nodded again. It didn't occur to me to be embarrassed. I was sure to flush if one of the boys at my school were to say I was pretty. I spent hours, each day, staring at the profile of Joseph, a chocolate brown beanpole of a boy who didn't know I was alive. On the other hand, Daddy's friends called me pretty or beautiful all the time. Mr. Parker, who owned Odyssey, one of the nightclubs where Daddy performed, sang Curtis Mayfield's "Miss Black America" whenever I walked into a room, but it never made me feel like a beauty queen with a sash across her chest and an armful of red roses.

The sun was hot that afternoon and I was lonely. Summer vacation was coming soon. Moving to Brooklyn, months after school already started, was practically a guarantee that I did not make any friends. Even the busybody girls, the ones who might adopt the new girl as a pet or a sidekick, couldn't be bothered to make the effort so late in the term. Come summer, everyone scattered and in September, new cliques formed again. Five schools in three years made me an expert on being the new kid and the precarious timing of making friends.

I was thinking about school and all the boys who never talked to me, while Edward babbled on about nothing at all. I could have cared less about what he was saying and I knew I should be getting home. But I didn't make a move.

Perhaps if I wasn't so close to Roger and Sammy, I might have wondered why a grown man, one of Daddy's friends, spent fifteen minutes talking to an eleven-year-old girl. But the thought never crossed my mind.

"It's hot," Edward said. "Do you want an ice cream cone?"

I looked across the street at the Baskin-Robbins. All thirty-one flavors seemed to be calling my name.

"Sure," I said.

"Hey, Manny," Edward called to a pair of legs sticking out from underneath a rusty blue VW Beetle. "I'll be right back."

He took my hand as we crossed the street, though I was certainly big enough to cross on my own. When we got to the other side, he did not let my hand go. This was all such a strange sequence of events that I began to forget I was there at all. I was an apparition, watching some other little girl meet a man, hold his hand, walk into the ice cream shop.

Edward asked me what flavor I wanted. I chose strawberry. Then he asked me if I always chose strawberry. I nodded yes.

"Well, then. Choose something else," he said. There was a teasing quality in his voice that I did not know how to place. He was still holding my hand.

I cast my eyes over the vast selection and, with a quick glance at the clock on the wall, I chose butter pecan.

Edward smiled and told the girl behind the counter, "Two butter pecans."

I looked at him and let the sides of my mouth curve upward. He'd chosen to have what I was having. What kind of grown-up did that?

Cones in hand, we crossed the street again.

"Thank you for the cone," I said. "But I better get home. My dad is waiting."

"How about a kiss on the cheek?" Edward said, kneeling down to my height. On close inspection, his cheek was stubbly, with razor bumps and ingrown hair. Just like my father's. When Mommy was still around, my father lay across her lap and she plucked his errant hairs with a pair of tweezers. When she was done, she held his face tenderly and they kissed. The tweezing, the kiss that followed, seemed to me the very essence of romance. Not what you did in public, onstage, when everyone was watching, but what happened later, after the curtain dropped and everyone went home. The real deal.

"Okay," I told Edward, kissing the cheek that was turned to me. "Bye."

"Come see me again," Edward said, waving.

♠

The ice cream seemed to melt faster than I could eat it, which I didn't mind. I didn't care much for the butter pecan flavor and regretted not choosing the strawberry instead. Then I heard Edward's voice in my head, cajoling me to choose something else. Thinking about how he chose butter pecan as well, at my suggestion, made my heart jump a little and I lengthened my stride. I took giant steps, trying to cover an entire sidewalk square every time my foot hit that ground. New York was strange that way, I thought. The buildings were so tall and big. But if you looked down when you walked, the way I did, everything seemed so small. The concrete was nothing but square after square, small galaxies I could span with the distance between two feet.

I liked to imagine that each square on the sidewalk represented some purpose that was just waiting for me to name. Maybe the squares were jump-rope arenas and, once a year, a million girls lined up from one end of Brooklyn to another, each girl in a square, in a race to see who could jump the longest, who could jump the fastest. Perhaps each block of the sidewalk represented a letter like the glowing boxes on *Wheel of Fortune.* I imagined turning each square around and discovering a word, then another word, a story without end. And by the time I got home, Edward was more than one hundred sidewalk boxes away and as distant a thought.

I began to stop by the garage every day after school. Edward could be counted on for treats. He asked me a few questions about school, then he asked for a kiss on the cheek. The other guys in the garage started to call me "Edward's little girlfriend" but he just waved them away. "Chups, man," he said, falling into Jamaican slang. "Y'all have no cut out."

Sometimes he held my hand. He declared my hands, like the rest of me, very pretty. "They're so small," he said, stretching his fingers out over mine. Even after he washed them, his hands still felt grainy; his fingernails held half-moons of oil that glistened like the white tips of a French manicure. I told Edward that I could see his was a dirty business and I marveled that Daddy let him near his cream leather interiors.

"Oh, no problem there, sweetheart," Edward said. "When I work on your daddy's car, I wear white gloves."

We were ten ice cream flavors and two weeks into our acquaintance when I told Daddy about Edward.

We were in the Mercedes on a Saturday afternoon. Daddy was pretending that the air-conditioning worked and I was roasting like a pig on a spit. We drove by the garage.

"Gee, Edward did a lousy job on this air conditioner," I said, holding my hand up to the vent and feeling warm air on my open palm.

"Who's Edward?" Daddy asked disinterestedly.

"Your friend at the garage," I told him.

Daddy looked at me with increased curiosity. "What friend? At what garage?"

I rolled my eyes. "You know who I mean."

Daddy was serious now. He trained both eyes on me and his foot dropped a little heavier on the gas pedal. "I'm telling you, I don't know who you're talking about." As he swung a wild left, cars blew their horns from every direction.

"Edward from down the street," I said. "He fixes your car."

"I get my car fixed in Queens," Daddy said. "Fucking hell. What did this guy say to you?"

"He said he was your friend and that he fixes your Mercedes," I said, looking out the window nervously. Now I was in trouble without it even being my fault. How was I supposed to know who fixed Daddy's car?

"He's nice, Daddy," I insisted. "He buys me ice cream sometimes."

"What??!!" Daddy roared, spinning the steering wheel toward me and pulling the car over to the side of the road. "What did I tell you about strangers?"

"He said he wasn't a stranger."

Daddy grabbed me by the collar. I was wearing my favorite dress. White, with different-colored polka dots and a pink Peter Pan collar and pink sleeves. Too much of a doll dress for a girl my age, but I still loved it. It was a birthday present from Mommy, the year before.

"Look, little girl," Daddy said, holding my face close to his. "What did I tell you about taking care of yourself on the street?"

"Don't talk to strangers," I repeated obediently. I could hear the quiver in my voice and the evidence of my own fear only made me more afraid. "But he wasn't a stranger. He said he was your friend!"

"Look, Angela," Daddy said, sinking back into his bucket seat, his hands moving up and down like a TV lawyer reviewing the evidence. "I'm going to ask you a question and I need you to tell me the truth. I'm not going to be mad at you. But I need to know the truth. Did this man ever touch you?"

I squirmed and didn't answer. I wanted to faint. On soap operas, whenever there was too much drama, the women fainted.

Daddy grabbed my face with both hands and looked me in the eye. "Did this guy touch you?"

I took a deep breath, tested Daddy's patience by rolling down the window and sucking in a lungful of warm, sticky air.

"Sometimes, he held my hand," I said. "And usually he asked me for a kiss—"

I didn't get to finish my sentence because Daddy was steaming. "Fucking hell," he fumed. "Son-of-a-bitch wants to mess with my little girl?"

Turning the car abruptly, he drove the wrong way down the one-way street. I held on to my seat, terrified, like being on a backward-facing carnival ride.

"Just on the cheek, Daddy, I swear." I began to sob.

"Don't defend him!" Daddy bellowed. "Don't fucking make excuses for that bastard. I just hope he's a Christian because when I'm done with him . . ."

Daddy screeched onto Tilden Avenue. All the cars around us began to honk. At the next intersection, Daddy ran through a stop sign. A man, crossing the street, jumped back and stuck his middle finger at us. Daddy jumped out of the car.

"Come fuck with me if you're bad," Daddy threatened as he walked around to the back. "Today is the wrong fucking day to test me." Daddy opened up the trunk of the car and took out the jack he used to change a flat tire. He began to swing the metal around, like a baseball bat. The man, who was bald with a stomach as round as his head, looked scared and backed away.

"Thought so," Daddy said, jumping back behind the wheel and spinning down Utica. I fastened my seat belt and prayed I would survive.

Daddy reached the garage in what felt like seconds. He pulled up to the first gas pump and leapt out of the car. I was frozen.

"Come on," Daddy said.

But I could not move. My legs were like blocks of ice and my heart was on fire. I looked at Daddy's bulging eyes and flaring nostrils. Somewhere along the way, he'd rolled up his sleeves and his fists were at the ready. Something bad was going to happen. Something violent and uncontrollably male. I wanted Mommy then, more than I ever did in the six months that she had been away. I was sure that only she could shield me from the bright light in my father's eyes.

♠

Daddy opened the passenger-side door, unlocked my seat belt, and lifted me, like an invalid, out of the car. He set me down in front of the garage.

"Show me which one," Daddy said, in a voice that attempted to be reasonable, but the words burned on his lips. He yanked me twenty paces to where the mechanics gathered. The smell of gasoline was stronger than I remembered it, the music louder. I looked carefully at the men working at the station, as if any of them might be Edward in disguise. Then I turned to Daddy and whispered, "He's not here. Let's go."

"Don't cover for him!" Daddy said, raising his hand as if he meant to smack me. I stumbled backward, in expectation of a blow that never came. Daddy put his hand down, and I recovered my balance.

My father walked over to the cassette player and shut it off. The garage was enveloped in silence. Five men stood before Daddy, in expectation and defiance. Daddy was fearless.

"One of you motherfuckers is messing with my little girl," he bellowed.

I wanted to protest, to explain that none of these men were the man that Daddy was looking for. But I was still waiting to be hit and I wasn't sure if, once he'd found Edward, he might not return to finish off with me. Daddy reached into his back pocket and pulled out his wallet. Without a moment's hesitation, he flashed a badge that I'd seen him buy at a magic and novelty shop.

"Allow me to introduce myself, gentlemen," Daddy said, taking a deep breath and slipping into his showman's voice. "My name is Officer Goodman and I'm with the Fifty-ninth Precinct. And when I find the motherfucker who's been touching my little girl, I'm not going to put him in jail, I'm going to put him under the motherfucking jail. The rest of you bums will be brought up on charges of aiding and abetting, which carry a minimum sentence of six to nine months. If you cooperate . . ."

Just then, we heard a toilet flush. The door closest to me parted and Edward opened it, grinning.

"Who turned off my music?" was the first thing he said.

Spying me, he smiled and added, "Hey there, pretty."

Daddy was on him before Edward could utter another word. He

slammed Edward against a wall of tools and pummeled his face with both fists.

"Do I know you, fool?" Daddy roared. "Do I know you? Telling my little girl that you my friend. I'm asking you, do I know you?"

Maybe the fake police badge impressed them or maybe the men figured Edward had earned Daddy's furious blows. But none of the men made a move to break up the fight, which seemed to last forever. Daddy rolled over Edward like he was the sea and Edward was a drowning man. Every time Edward seemed to steady himself and held his head up again, Daddy knocked him down. Daddy threw punch after punch until finally Edward fell against his chest, slid down Daddy's unbruised frame, and mercifully hit the floor.

One day shortly before Mommy left, we were grocery shopping when she stopped in the middle of the street. It was early Sunday morning, that in-between time when the church folks are getting prayed up and the Saturday night sinners are still in bed, laid up. The streets were empty although the shops were beginning to open. We turned the corner and saw two white police officers frisking two young black men. The boys' legs were spread open and their arms were in a V shape against the concrete, as if they were spidermen, ready to crawl right up the wall. Mommy told me to stand back, and for a second I thought she might pull a gun out of her massive curls like Pam Grier's packing Afro in *Foxy Brown*.

Mommy stopped a hundred feet away from the cops and the boys, folded her arms, and said nothing.

"Keep moving, lady," the first officer said. He was small and wiry, with dark hair. "Police business."

"Oh yeah?" Mommy said, her voice even but firm. "Well, these young brothers are my neighbors so that makes it my business."

"I could drag you down to the courthouse for obstructing justice," said the other cop. He was taller than the first guy, with the kind of physique that seemed to fluctuate somewhere between husky and fat. Then he nodded his head over toward me. "Take your little girl down there too, if you want."

Mommy took two giant steps back and crossed her arms again. "I'm not trying to interfere with your business. I just want you to know that I'm watching. I'm watching both of you."

The officers rolled their eyes, frisked the boys, then let them go.

"You know, the next time someone grabs your purse or your old man knocks you upside your head, don't call us," the first police officer said. "Okay, lady?"

Mommy looked for a second like she might drop-kick the officer, then suddenly she looked as if she might cry. Maybe she couldn't make up her mind. Then she smiled broadly at the officers and said, "Have a nice day, gentlemen."

♠

Later, when my father heard the story, he called Mommy a damn fool. "What were you going to do if one of those cops took out a gun?" he asked.

"Bear witness," Mommy said.

"And what if he shot you or Angela?" my father asked. He was on his feet, pacing. His face was flushed and his Adam's apple bobbed so furiously, it seemed like his heart was beating in his throat.

"Teddo, it's 1979. You should know by now that the black people's revolution isn't about the Panthers and an army rising up. It's about us loving each other, it's about bearing witness and speaking the truth."

♠

As I watched Daddy beat Edward, I prayed that something in my silent posture was reminiscent of Mommy staring down those cops, that underneath my doing nothing there was some higher good. When Mommy was around, I never doubted that as I made my way to womanhood, I was growing up to be like her: black, beautiful, bold. I trusted that each day, each month, each year provided new lessons and that if I watched carefully, I'd learn all I needed to know. Ever since she was gone, the path that once seemed so sure, slowly disappeared. I'd followed the trail of crumbs into the woods, but then there was no more trail, just wolves at every turn. I knew that Daddy thought he could save me, that he'd be the Prince Charming to rescue the lost little girl. But as I watched him beat the daylights out of Edward, I was reminded that if I rubbed him the wrong way, Daddy was fully capable of being a wolf, too.

Daddy started to walk away when Edward moaned something that sounded like "Angela," but could well have been "Aaaaaggggh." Daddy spun on his heels, went over to Edward's slumped body, and began kicking him in the stomach.

"Don't you say her name!" Daddy screamed. "Don't you ever say her name. Don't look at her and if you find yourself on the same street as her, you better cross. Because the next time I see you, I'm coming with my gun, you miserable piece of shit."

Daddy kept kicking Edward and he did not stop until Edward began to cough up blood. Then he kicked him once again, across the forehead, and turned to me.

Edward's face was bloody and bruised and I stood there for a second, wondering what I could do. I wanted to say something, but what? Thanks for the ice cream? Thanks for being my friend?

"Come on, Angela," Daddy said. "It's time to go."

Filthy and sweaty, his hands covered with either Edward's blood or his own, Daddy opened the trunk of the Mercedes and took out a towel. He covered the front seat with it. Then he got into the car and we drove away.

♠

The next morning, Daddy announced that he was walking me to school. "You're going to take a new route," he said. "I don't want you going anywhere near that gas station."

Quietly, I followed Daddy out the front door. Instead of turning right as I usually did on the way to school, we turned left. Daddy led me down several blocks of pretty tree-lined streets with big Victorian-style houses. By the time we'd gotten to school, all we'd done was make a big circle around the gas station.

The problem was, by the end of the school day, I couldn't remember which way to go. Without familiar neighbors or friends to distinguish them, every brownstone, every side street looked exactly the same. It seemed so simple in the morning that I did not bother to write any of it down. I followed one group of rowdy kids who I thought lived on my block, but they took me away from the pretty streets to a tower of project-style apartments, where they vanished inside. I didn't know what to do. I didn't want to ask a kid and risk getting picked on, or worse. I didn't want to ask a grown-up; every time I closed my eyes, even for a second, Edward's bloody face floated like a jack-o'-lantern before me. Finally, I asked an old woman pushing a cart of laundry. She gave me directions that, with a few small glitches, eventually led me home. By the time I opened the front door I was more than an hour late.

Daddy was sitting at the kitchen table, the telephone, a pad, and pen in front of him.

"You're late," he said quietly.

"I got lost," I explained, exhausted. "I couldn't remember the way home."

"Did you go to see him?" Daddy asked, the venom in his voice unmistakable.

"Edward?" I asked, incredulous. "Of course not."

He jumped out of his chair and pinned me against the wall. "I'm only going to ask you one more time, Angela. Did you go and see him?"

I was so afraid, fully aware that the truth did not set me free. My father's breath was hot on my face and I could not look him in his fiery eyes. His fists kept me flat against the wall; my shoulders quivered and threatened to crack. I waited for the hit, my turn at the receiving end of Daddy's anger. But it never came. I knew then that it was not a fine line that kept Daddy from flattening me like a bug, but a web of lines, burned on my forehead like the image of an invisible tattoo.

"You know he's not your friend," Daddy said, releasing the pressure on my shoulders, his voice shaking. "I don't care how many ice cream cones he bought you. I don't know what could have happened if I hadn't . . . if I hadn't intervened." I flashed then to Daddy's punishing blows, to Edward spitting blood across the oil-stained garage floor.

"I know, Daddy," I said, leaning in to give him a kiss then recoiling slightly at the sight of his stubbly cheek, so much like Edward's. Frightened by the similarity, I gave him a hug instead.

"You don't know, baby," Daddy said, reaching for the newspaper. "You should read the papers, Angela. You should read the paper and see what I'm trying to protect you from."

♠

On Tuesday, May 19, the headline of the *Amsterdam News* read: THE KILLING FIELDS. The picture was of a playground and a body bag and a bicycle propped against a tree. A caption underneath the photograph said, "14-year-old Eric Middlebrooks found dead, near his home. The Atlanta child murders continue."

I read the story with a scared helplessness. I felt bad because I knew that was how I was supposed to feel, but I didn't know what to do with the warning that someday the kid in the newspaper might be me.

"There are more kids, plenty more," my father said, hopping to his feet and taking off for his bedroom. Seconds later, he returned with a manila envelope full of newspaper clippings. He spread them out on the table and raised his eyebrows at me. Evidence. He pulled up a chair next to mine and together we sat and read the stories. A boy named Hope and a boy named Bell. The karate-loving kid, who disappeared on his way to see a martial arts movie downtown. Boys who died on errands for their mothers, one to pay a bill, the other to buy his mom a pack of cigarettes. Then the first girl found, same age as me, hanging from a tree with a pair of panties that did not belong to her, stuffed in her mouth.

"The worst thing is that the police aren't doing anything about it," Daddy said, putting his arm around me. "If the kids are poor, they say it's drugs. If a bike is stolen, they say it's a robbery. They blame the parents; one of those boys' fathers is still a suspect. Do you know what kind of defense I have if something happens to you? None. Do you know what they will do to me if you ever go missing?"

My father did not answer his own question, but began to shake then in a way that made me wonder what was worse, the prospect of losing me or bearing the blame. My father made dinner and I listened to his theories about the identity of the murderer: a crazed member of the Ku Klux Klan, some government organization performing medical experiments on black children, just like the Tuskegee experiments, or a homicidal sexual pervert. He did not say it, but I understood that he considered Edward to be an example of the last category, in thought if not deed, and more than worthy of the pounding he received.

We ate our omelets silently, as if our kitchen was a morgue.

When the dishes were done, we went back to the articles, my father insisting that I read each one aloud. It took hours to get through them, nearly two dozen clips describing fear and frustration, pages and pages of loss. And when we were done, I knew that my definition on tragedy had shifted. I had lost my mother. She was gone. But I was not a missing child. I had not lost myself.

The Anthem and Its Uses

school was out

and Daddy's summer season was shaping up to be a lucrative one. There were lots of birthday parties scheduled, a few mini mall openings, and the most lucrative gigs of all, country clubs and resort hotels. Of all the resorts where my father performed, Daddy liked Grossinger's the best. Most of the other places made their contracts hourly and Daddy drove half the night to come home and sleep. Grossinger's put Daddy up for the night, so he usually brought me along for the ride. The manager, Harry, even invited us to eat dinner in the dining room.

That Friday afternoon turned out to be the perfect day for a drive in the country. The weather was warm, but at fifty miles an hour on the freeway, the air blew cool on our faces. Daddy was dressed in a suit, though he took off the jacket and laid it across the backseat. I was wearing a new white Izod shirt Daddy bought me and a pair of green plaid Bermuda shorts that Mommy bought the summer before.

"You look great," Daddy said. "Just like one of those little girls at the country club."

"I thought you liked me better in kente cloth," I said devilishly.

"It's okay," Daddy said, fiddling with the radio station. "Sometimes you got to go along to get along. At least your hair isn't relaxed."

Once we got off the thruway, I kept my eye out for the first farm that we drove past. I did a silent nod to the white barn with the white tin roof that I always looked out for. That old barn was my secret lucky thing. I studied the houses that dotted the road along our way: the stone cottages, the newer houses with the wraparound porches, the red barns that numbered more than a dozen before we reached Grossinger's itself. The Catskills made me feel like I was Laura Ingalls Wilder and it took all my strength not to call my father "Pa." Driving upstate made it easy to pretend Mommy was not gone. She was simply waiting for us in a pale-green farmhouse, just over the hill.

"What kind of people live around here?" I asked my father.

"Not a lot of black people, I can tell you that."

"No, I mean, what kind of people are they? I see a lot of land. Are they farmers?"

My father shook his head. "No, not anymore. There's a lot of people from New York up here. A lot of these houses are second homes."

I'd never heard the term before and the whole rest of the way I kept imagining what it meant to have a second home. Did that mean you owned two sets of dishes, one in each house? Two beds? Two toothbrushes? Did two homes mean two of everything? More than money, it seemed to me that people with a second home must have more joy, more stability, more love than I ever knew. When Mommy called us, when she and my father got divorced, would I also have a second home?

We drove past a field of girls running around in little plaid skirts and waving sticks in the air.

"What are they doing?" I asked my father.

"I don't know," he said. "Why don't we go and find out?"

"Won't you be late?"

"It's just past noon," my father said, looking at the clock on the dashboard. "We've got all afternoon to set up for tonight's show."

"But I want to swim in the pool," I said.

My father swung the car into the field parking lot. "You'll have plenty of time to swim."

♦

I got out of the car and my white skippies felt weird pressing into the grass. My father wasn't much for the great outdoors; I couldn't remember the last time we even walked in a park.

"You look great," my father said again, with a nervousness I did not understand. "I'm so glad you wore that outfit."

Watching the game, I felt as if I'd been plopped into some kind of interview. We took a seat in the bleachers, away from the other families. There were about twenty people watching the game and they were all white. One of the girls on the field was black, though, and I did not need to see my father's face to know he was staring at her as intensely as I was. She was fair-skinned with brown curly hair and shimmering blond streaks. She looked a little like Stacy Lattisaw or a young Lena Horne.

The girls ran back and forth across the field and, now that we were closer, I could see little nets at the top of their sticks. They caught and threw the ball with their sticks; I liked the serious expressions on their faces. At my school the girls were showoffs at basketball, yelling "Swish" every time they made a basket. I didn't understand the game on the field, but it seemed like there was some kind of secret strategy at hand, like chess. I was into that.

One of the mothers walked a crying baby back and forth behind the bleachers. When he quieted, she walked over to us.

"Hi, I'm Alison," she said, extending her hand to my father. She had dark hair and was wearing a floral print dress and white sneakers.

My father shook her hand and introduced the both of us.

"Do you play lacrosse, Angela?" Alison asked and I could tell from Daddy's expression that, like me, he thanked her silently for the information. I thought then I'd figured it out. Daddy was running a game of three-card monte and Alison was an easy mark.

"No, I've never played lacrosse," I answered.

"But she's always wanted to," Daddy piped in.

"You should meet my daughter, Sarah," Alison said, and she took a seat next to Daddy.

I watched her through the game for any jive turkey Danita moves. But she just rocked the baby back and forth (his name was Jesse) and cheered when the team in green plaid skirts scored.

Twenty minutes later, the game was over and the black girl

walked right up to us. She gave Alison a kiss on the cheek and said, "Hey, Mom."

Both Daddy and I tried to play it cool.

"Great game," he said. Mommy used to say that my father could sell ice to the Eskimos and she made it clear that this was no compliment. But watching my father with Alison and Sarah, I wished that I could channel just a little bit of his magic.

"Yeah, great game," I said, looking down at the ground.

"Are you thinking about applying to the Holyoke School?" Sarah asked me.

I shrugged.

"We're looking at a few schools in the area," Daddy said, and I almost fell out. What was he talking about?

"Sarah, why don't you give Teddo and Angela a little tour?" Alison said cheerfully.

"Well," she said, pulling her sweat-stained shirt away from herself. "If you can bear the funk, I'd be glad to."

I smiled, and it felt like the most natural thing in the world. Sarah was cool, real cool.

◆

She led us behind the gatehouse and we saw that the Holyoke School was as big as a college campus. There was a lower school, a middle school, and an upper school. It was all girls and was nearly a hundred years old. We saw a building that looked like a gigantic treehouse and Sarah explained that inside there was a maze of classrooms. "It's the new science center," she said. "We're all pretty excited about it." There was a fancy dance studio that was all glass. Inside, the ceilings were as high as a church and we could see ourselves, reflected in a huge mirror on the opposite wall. We stood outside for a few moments, me and Daddy, Alison, Sarah, and the baby. We watched the girls in identical leotards and tights, six of them standing at the bar in the center of the room, their legs jutting up and down.

Sarah said that the architect came from Paris and then she apologized for not remembering his name.

"No biggie," I said.

Daddy was his usual chatty self, enthralling Alison and Sarah with stories about his magic show. But honestly, I couldn't remember the last time I'd exchanged more than ten words with a girl my own age.

"Are you the only black girl?" Daddy asked. I wondered if Sarah and Alison would be offended, since clearly Sarah was mixed. But they didn't seem to mind.

"No, there are about twelve of us," Sarah explained.

"What grade are you in?" I asked.

"Eighth," Sarah said. "I'll be going into the upper school next year. How about you?"

"I just finished sixth grade," I said. "I'll be in seventh next year."

"That's right," Alison said. "City schools get out earlier than the schools up here."

"You're so lucky." Sarah grinned at me.

♦

At the end of the tour, my father and Alison exchanged phone numbers. Alison said that if I decided to apply, my father and I should stay with them when I came up for my interview. I did not know how my father did it. One minute he was going on about white devils and the original Asiatic black man's place as the rightful heir of the earth, the next he was acting like there'd be no better place for me to go than a straight-up preppy white boarding school in the country. He was always telling me that black women were the most beautiful women on earth, and that I was his Miss Black America, but he dated Danita and looked like he wanted to date Alison, too. How could race anger my father so and, at the same time, he managed to act so at home around white folks and black folks alike?

I had my own quandaries. I'd never been to Disneyland, but I imagined I'd feel the same way about it as I did about the Catskills: a fun and enchanting place that you visited, but where no one really lived. After meeting Sarah and Alison though, after seeing how beautiful the Holyoke School was, I wondered if I'd been wrong. Could I go to a school like that? Could I be one of those people with a second home?

"Nice school," my father said, finally.

"Yeah," I said, staring out the window. "I bet it cost a gazillion dollars."

My father reached behind my ear and pulled out a quarter. "So what, you're practically made of money!"

I laughed then and we both let it go. My father popped an Ashford and Simpson tape in and began to sing along. I looked at the rolling scenery with new eyes. In my head, I heard Sarah's voice say again and again, "You're so lucky. You're so lucky." She'd only been talking about my school getting out early, but she planted the seed of an idea I was anxious to see grow. Was I? Could I be? I liked the sound of it. Lucky.

♦

When we arrived at the lodge, Harry greeted us cheerfully. "You brought the good weather with you!" he said. "We've got a beautiful pool. Why don't you take advantage of the pool?" Harry was careful to make the offer, but Daddy never took him up on it. But after the first couple of times that I visited Grossinger's, I never came up without my bathing suit. Daddy never swam anywhere, not even at the beach. Mommy, who taught me, told me that

Daddy almost drowned when he was my age. She used to say that my father had a fear of water so deep only God could fix it.

That afternoon, before his evening performance, I swam in the pool while Daddy sat on a lounge chair. He was reading a book about Houdini and he was wearing a dark green linen suit. All the other fathers were wearing polo shirts and chinos, but Daddy was wearing a suit. He took the jacket off, but only because we were poolside. The minute I was done swimming, he cheerfully threw me a towel and put his jacket on again.

On the way back to our room, I asked him why he never wore casual clothes like the other dads and he just looked at me sideways, like I was four feet two inches of pure stupid piled on his doorstep.

"A suit commands respect," he said.

"You have to command respect at the pool?" I asked, incredulous.

Daddy's broad lips began to tremble and I could see the sweat glistening on his nose. "A black man can't afford to relax!" he glowered. "Let me come down there in shorts and a T-shirt and those same white people will be asking me to fetch them towels and get them a cool drink."

I just shook my head. No matter where we were or what we were doing, everything came down to race. Daddy's guard was up.

"I thought you liked it here?" I whined.

"Hmmm," Daddy snorted. "I don't 'like' it anywhere except maybe Africa."

"You've never been to Africa!"

"That's where my people are from. How am I not going to like it there? That's like telling a baby that it's not going to like its mommy's womb."

"Speaking of mommys—" I began.

"Don't start," Daddy warned me.

"Have you heard any news about mine?"

"No," Daddy said, as he opened the door to our small hotel room.

"Would you tell me if you did?"

"Yes," he said emphatically. Which was how I recognized his lie. Daddy liked to talk. He only used one-word answers when he was trying to avoid the truth.

I plopped on the second double bed. "Maybe I should write her?" I asked in a small voice. I was trying not to start an argument, but Daddy blew up anyway.

"Why do you want to write her??!" he roared as if I was writing away for a free membership to hell. "Don't I take care of you? Don't I clothe and feed you? She's the devil who left us. We don't need her!"

He stomped over to the window and yanked the curtain backward. "Look at where we are! The Catskill Mountains. How many black children do you know spend their summer swimming in the pool with a view of beautiful mountains like this?"

I looked over toward the window and tried to make the ache of missing Mommy go away. But Daddy wanted an answer to his question.

"None, Daddy," I whispered, fingering the fringe of the nubby blue pillowcase.

"How many black children do you see in this resort, besides you?"

"None, Daddy."

"Instead of writing your no-good Mommy who up and left us in a lurch, you should be writing me a thank-you letter for being such a good father," he fumed. "Not many men could do what I've done—raise a child for close to a year on their own. And a girl child at that!"

I laid my head back on the pillow as Daddy continued his rant about how ungrateful I was, how misguided my affections. I thought about how Houdini used to do a trick called the Water Torture Cell. In the trick, his ankles were tied together and he was locked into a water tank, upside down. Daddy said that the trick was some crazy white boy shit. But listening to Daddy hold forth, I imagined myself diving facedown into the pool. My lips pressed toward the tile floor and my ankles skimming the water's surface. Even if my ankles were braced, I didn't doubt that I could get free. Dry land and the terrain of Daddy's mind frightened me. I was just beginning to understand that my father was a magic trick I could never escape.

"You should be thanking me! Not questioning me about her!" he continued at full blast, oblivious to the fact that I was hardly listening to him at all. "Matter of fact, that's what I want you to do. Sit down and write me a thank-you letter."

He bolted over to the hotel desk, took out a piece of hotel stationery, and slammed it on the desk. He pulled a pen out of his suit pocket and slammed that down as well. "Hard as I work," he muttered. "I deserve a little praise."

Then he pulled out the chair and motioned for me to sit. Tired and trembling, I did.

He sat down on top of the desk, leaning forward, his face just inches from my own. His expression was maddeningly blank. I did not know if he was about to spit on me or kiss me. When he spoke, his voice was soft again.

"Doesn't have to be long. Just has to be sincere."

Then he got up, walked to the door of our room and said, "I'm going to get a drink."

When he left, I picked up the pen, torn between two desires. Part of me wanted to soothe his bruised ego. The other part of me wanted to write him a very sincere note telling him to loosen up, get a real job, stop being such a racist, and while he was at it, tell me where Mommy was. I knew my father. He was too much of a conspiracy theorist not to know where she was. No way in hell could he be keeping track of all the places where the CIA was destabilizing governments in Africa and Latin America and not be keeping tracking of Mommy as well.

But for all my closet bravado, it didn't take me five minutes to decide which letter I was going to write.

Dear Daddy,
I am very sorry I am such an ungrateful daughter. You buy my clothes and my food. You bring me to beautiful places like the Catskills where I can swim in a lovely pool.

I paused, then continued.

You educate me about Afro-American history and give me pride in myself as a black woman.

He might think I was being rude if I called myself a "woman." I crossed it out and replaced it with "girl."

All of my friends have fathers with boring jobs. Only my father is a prestidigitator. I never cease to be amazed by your magic tricks. I am honored to be your daughter. You truly are the greatest.

Love,
Angela

I folded the letter carefully, then put it in an envelope which I sealed. I scrawled Daddy's name across the front and placed the letter on his pillow. Then I crawled into bed, pretending to be asleep when Daddy came back in to get ready for his show. When I was little, Mommy never read me bedtime stories out of books. She told me tall tales instead. These were family stories that she'd learned from her great-grandmother who'd come from Louisiana. I once asked her why we never went to Louisiana. She said all the old folks died and that everybody young came north, to Chicago or New York. "No reason to go down South and chase ghosts," she'd say. But after Mommy left, my father said that one day we'd drive cross-country, from New York to Nevada. He said we'd stop and visit the places our people were from and we'd take the same Route 66 that Nat King Cole sang about. Daddy said that we'd stop in Vegas and catch a show at the Sands, maybe Diana Ross or Richard Pryor. He said that one day, when he was rich and famous, he'd get a contract at the Sands and we'd live in the hotel for a whole month.

◆

When Mommy started telling a tall tale, she started the story the same way. "One time, not yours or my time, but a bygone time . . ." Then she'd continue the story about how some slaves just flew like birds off a ship and back to Africa or about how a girl who dreamed of being a princess wrapped herself in cat skin and outwitted her fate. But my favorite fairy tale was one she called "Woman and Man Started Even." One time, Mommy told me, not my time or your time, but in a bygone time, man and woman were perfectly even. They knew the same amount of fancy words. They could solve a puzzle, any puzzle, in the exact same amount of time. If they ran a race, they crossed the finish line together, not a hair apart. Then one day, man snuck away and asked God for more strength. He came back, all big and muscular, and started bossing woman around. But she wasn't having it. *She* snuck away and asked God for something so she and man could be even. God gave her all the keys to the house. She locked up the kitchen, she locked up the bed-room. She locked up the room where the children slept. When man came home from work, he was straight out of luck and he knew it. No matter how much he shook the doors of the house, the locks did not give. The woman just sat on the porch, sipping a cold lemonade and dangling her keys. "Always remember that," Mommy said. "Man may have the strength but woman has the keys to the house."

I used my power to keep my eyes shut and my body perfectly still when my father came in to change for his show. I listened to his breathing; I smelled the alcohol when he walked in and the toothpaste when he walked out. I felt him kiss me on the cheek before he left, and I tried not to be mad. In times like this, when my father and I were sorrier than two dirty socks forgotten behind an old heaving washing machine, I wondered if Mommy was somewhere in California, sitting on a porch and rocking in a comfy chair. Was she out there, sipping a nice cold lemonade and dangling the keys to our hearts?

The next morning, Daddy was cheerful. I woke to find him sitting on the side of my bed and smiling.

"Thank you for the lovely letter, sweetie," he said, beaming. As if he hadn't ordered me to write it under the threat of God knows what.

"You're welcome, Daddy," I said, mimicking his sunny tone.

"Come on, take a shower and get dressed," he said as he jumped to his feet. "We've got to roll."

I took my clothes from Daddy's overnight bag and went into the bathroom. Outside, I could hear my father fussing with the radio dial, then singing along to Marvin Gaye. "Don't go and talk about my father," he sang. "God is my friend . . ."

A few minutes later, Daddy rapped on the bathroom door.

"It doesn't come off, you know." He chuckled.

"What?" I called from beneath the shower's powerful jets.

"All that beautiful blackness, it doesn't come off." He laughed again. "So get a move on, Miss Black America. I'll be late for my next show."

On our way out of town, we passed the same PX Mart, with its red-and-black logo and the marquee sign out front that said: BEST SUBS IN TOWN. I never got a chance to taste them. Daddy did not buy anything but prepackaged food when we were in the mountains. "I don't want any of these country white folk making me a sandwich," he said. So on the way home from the Catskills, he bought us Cokes and Pringles, but that was it. No hot food until we reached a McDonald's halfway down the thruway.

That morning, our drive was even longer than usual because we weren't going home to Brooklyn. Daddy was performing at a birthday party in northern New Jersey.

In the car, Daddy quizzed me on black history.

"Who was the first black woman to run for president?"

"Shirley Chisholm."

"What year was that?"

"1972."

"Who was the first black person in Congress?"

"Blanche Bruce, Republican, Mississippi."

"What year was that?"

"1875."

"When was the next black representative elected?"

"1969."

The questions went on for miles, until Daddy got bored and popped in an old Al Green tape. Daddy said black music was history, too.

Al Green was busy singing to some sister about how he was still in love, still in love with her, when Daddy said, "I talked to Harry about that school."

"The Holyoke School?" I asked, as if we really were visiting a number of schools the way Daddy led Alison to believe.

"Harry says it's a great school, one of the first private boarding schools in the North to integrate."

I was scared then. Daddy did not run down a race history of a place unless he was thinking seriously about it.

"And it cost a gazillion dollars, don't forget," I said. I wasn't ready to get my hopes up about science centers in treehouses, lacrosse, and dance studios like churches. I had space in my heart for only one impossible dream at a time and that space was fully occupied.

"Harry says there are plenty of scholarships for a smart girl like you."

"I'm not that smart," I countered.

"Smart enough," my father said.

Then it hit me.

He'd had enough. Mommy was gone and my father was tired of having to do everything. Maybe he wanted me to go away. I wanted to ask him, but I didn't know how to ask the question or whether I could take the answer.

"Do you really want to send me away, Daddy?" I asked.

"No, princess," he said. "Never."

It wasn't true. We both knew it. Not because my father didn't love me, but because my mother taught us that words like "forever" and "always" and "never" were as slippery as a pair of Houdini's handcuffs.

♦

We arrived at Daddy's next gig, a huge white colonial on a *Leave It to Beaver* street, in the late afternoon. The porch was festooned with streamers and a huge sign said, "Happy Birthday, Seth."

Daddy rang the doorbell and a pretty woman with dark, curly hair and dimples answered the door.

"You must be the magician," she said. "Teddo, isn't it? I'm Mrs. Winterson."

A little bell went off in my head. She called Daddy by his first name, then expected him to use her last name. Daddy hated that.

He smiled broadly anyway and extended his hand. "How do you do? This is my daughter, Angela."

She shook Daddy's hand and smiled down at me. "Why don't you come around back? That's where the kids are." Then she pointed to a path that led around the side of the house.

The alarm bells were ringing wildly then. She didn't invite us into the house. Daddy was going to be hell to calm down later.

"Well, certainly then," Daddy said in his best Gomer Pyle voice, a fake smile plastered on his face. I followed him out back and prayed that the kids weren't monsters.

The show seemed to go well. He made a card rise out of the deck by itself and a dollar bill float in the air. Then he brought me into the act.

"One day, I bought my daughter, Angela, a coloring book," he began, lifting a coloring book to eye level. "There she is, in the back. Wave hello, Angela."

All thirty kids turned around and I waved. They waved back enthusiastically. I was too old to play with coloring books, could hardly remember a time when I did, but I liked when Daddy pointed me out to the crowd, linking me to his magic.

"But when I got home," Daddy continued, "I realized something was terribly wrong. The coloring book had all blank pages." He fanned the pages of the book and showed that every single one of them was as white as typewriter paper.

"But that's the benefit of having a father who's a magician,"

Daddy continued. "Because I reached into my pocket and pulled out my magic pen." He took a marker out of his pocket and held it up to the cover of the coloring book. Without touching it, he began to draw pictures in the air.

"Sooner than you can say 'Abracadabra,' there were beautiful pictures in my little girl's coloring book," Daddy said, fanning the pages of the book once again, to show drawing after drawing of an Indian circus and all its participants.

"But a few minutes later, I heard my baby girl crying," Daddy continued. "I said, 'What's the matter?' She said, 'Daddy, you forgot to buy crayons.' What was I going to do? It was getting late and the store was closed. So I reached up to the sky and I pulled down all the colors of the rainbow." Daddy made an elaborate gesture of pulling invisible colors, like streamers, down from the sky.

"Then I waved my handful of rainbow colors over the book," Daddy said, waving his hand over the book, his motion as graceful as a hula dancer. "And when I was done, my beautiful little girl had a spectacularly colored coloring book."

He flipped the pages again, and the kids oohed and aahed with each Technicolor page. Then Daddy recruited the birthday boy as his assistant and together they did a farrago of coin tricks: a bite out of the quarter, chop suey, scotch and soda. He was just wrapping up with the disappearing doves, when a middle-aged father, sipping a beer, began to heckle him.

"Bah," the man grumbled loudly. "No such thing as magic. I've seen five-year-olds do better."

Hecklers made me nervous, but Daddy did not seem to mind.

"Well, sir," Daddy said pleasantly. "If you're so sure this isn't magic, why don't you come right up to the front for this last trick? The closer you get, the less you can see and that is guaranteed by me."

"Now he's a poet," the guy sneered, striding up to the front of the lawn where Daddy stood. "If you're such a good magician, why don't you make yourself white?"

The world was still then. At least, that's how I remember it. The mouths of the other parents lay on the ground where they fell. The children were eerily still, cross-legged and kneeling, their heads and bodies twisted in the gestures of conversation. The dog lurched forward: mid-jump, mid-bark.

Daddy stood in front of his audience as I sat in the back. Our eyes met and, for an instant, it seemed that we levitated toward each other—our bodies floating in the open sky. When we met, we embraced. Daddy hugged me tightly and I pressed my hands against his burning face.

"It's all right," he whispered in my ear.

"I know," I whispered back.

When the world came alive again, the man was still there, the sting of his words fresh like spit on his lips.

"That's the wrong question, my brother," Daddy answered, slipping a little bit from his accentless magician's voice into the soulful slang of Marvin Gaye. "See, I was supposed to be white like you, but I made myself this color. That's why they call it that old black magic."

Then Daddy began singing. "That old black magic has me in a spell. That old black magic that I know so well . . ."

He just kept on singing and when he reached the second chorus, he began to dance a little Sammy Davis Jr. two-step. That's when I knew the sun had fallen out of the sky. Daddy hated Sammy Davis; he accused him of cooning. But there Daddy was: singing and dancing and when he was finished, he took a dramatic bow. The kids, confused, clapped halfheartedly. But their parents, clearly relieved, picked up the slack.

Afterward, the Wintersons invited us into the house. They

were all apologies as they offered us a seat at the long mahogany dining table.

Daddy refused. "We've got to be on our way," he said, fake smile firmly in place.

"I'd like to make this up to you," Mr. Winterson said, reaching for his checkbook.

"Money couldn't do it," Daddy said, his eyes trained on me.

"We really are very sorry," Mrs. Winterson said. She looked at Daddy anxiously as if he might break something in anger, or worse, return with picket signs and a crowd from the NAACP.

"Good day," Daddy said, taking my hand and walking toward the front door.

Seconds later, we were in the car and Daddy breathed a sigh of relief.

"I can't believe what that man said!" I cried out, the minute the engine started revving.

"I don't want to talk about it," Daddy said, staring straight ahead.

"What a racist man!" I continued, trying to egg Daddy on. I figured a healthy rant and rave about the evils of the white man might cheer Daddy up.

"I don't want to talk about this ever again," Daddy said, speaking softly but looking at me sternly. "Don't you ever mention that man or this day to me ever again."

I nodded as I frantically rustled through the stack of eight-tracks in the glove compartment. "Do you want to hear some Aretha, Daddy? How about some Curtis Mayfield?"

Daddy was silent for a moment. Then he said, "I'd rather if you sang."

"What should we sing?"

"The Negro National Anthem," he answered. "And not us, just you."

Daddy never asked me to sing by myself before. Compared to his smooth baritone, my voice was wobbly and uneven. But I knew that he didn't so much need for me to hit the right notes as he needed the healing power of the words.

So I sang:

> Lift ev'ry voice and sing, Till earth and heaven ring.
> Ring with the harmonies of liberty.
> Let our rejoicing rise, high as the list'ning skies,
> Let it resound loud as the rolling sea,
> Sing a song full of the faith that the dark past has taught us.
> Sing a song full of the hope that the present has brought us;
> Facing the rising sun of our new day begun,
> Let us march on till victory is won.

When I was done, Daddy asked me to sing it again. Then again, once more. We crossed the George Washington Bridge that way; Daddy staring straight ahead and me singing as sweetly as I could manage. As the car rolled across the steel girders of the bridge, it was like New Jersey was hell and Manhattan was heaven and we'd made it through the pearly gates. Together.

The Joy Is in the Waking

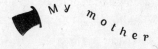 used to be part of my father's act, back when my father was calling himself "the African Khruse." He wore a gold turban with a red ruby. My mother wore a purple sari. An Indian woman came over to teach my mother how to do the dance of the scarves. I was so amazed by their breasts, their hips,

their bellies. We were all laughing, except for my father who sat in the corner silently, smoldering at my mother. When the music ended, he'd bark out, "Do it again. She still doesn't have it. Try it again." Hours later, no one was laughing and no one was smiling, and when my father hit the rewind button for the hundreth time, my mother ripped the scarf off her face. Tears turned her kohl-lined eyes muddy and her voice, choked with sobs, was as thick as a swamp. "I can't do it another time," she said. "I feel like a whore." Then she ran into the bedroom.

My father apologized to the woman and walked her to the front door. Then he followed my mother into the bedroom, their voices curried in anger. I heard glass breaking, pounding against the wall, whispering and crying. Then silence. When the sounds stopped and I was certain they weren't coming out again, I went into my bedroom, closed the door, and opened my dictionary. I looked up the word my mother used: whore.

My father worked alone after that. Though when my mother was still around, he'd get into these moods where he was convinced that my mother's modesty was the one thing holding him back from the big time. "Every great magician has an assistant," my father said, lobbing his disappointment across the dinner table. "It brings in the crowds, Melanie." My mother lifted a forkful of food to her mouth, chewed that one bite for what seemed like an endless amount of time, then answered my father with a voice that was as low and venomous, "You know what you can do with the crowds, Teddo."

After my mother left, my father seemed to take to the idea of being a solo act, in more ways than one. "If you want something done right, you've got to do it yourself," he muttered, practicing a particularly difficult trick. "Ain't nobody looking out for me, but me," he mumbled as he cracked eggs for our breakfast. "It's okay," he'd say, as he slid an omelet—yellow, unbroken, perfect—out of the pan and onto the plate. "I got this. I'm about to handle my business."

For almost nine months, since my mother left, my father did handle his business—more or less. I missed her, but I was becoming accustomed, even attached, to my father; he was like the nearsighted boy you start to depend on when your fiancé has gone off to war. I thought my father was comfortable with performing solo until the day he came home and announced that he'd incorporated me—more like drafted me, really—into his act. It was a little after nine; I was eating a TV dinner and watching *Good Times*, my favorite show.

After my mother left, our diet consisted almost exclusively of four things. Coca-Cola—my father drank two liters of it a day and was so fanatic about it that he'd get furious if I'd touched his supply. I was given my own two-liter, my name scratched across the red-and-white label with a black Sharpie. Then there were omelets, which my father ate two or three times a day. "It's a very sophisticated meal. Ask somebody French," he said. As if there were any French people living in Flatbush.

The third food group in our household was Pringles. My father positioned the tall cylinders of potato chips in strategic locations with all the care and concern of an asthmatic making sure there was always an inhaler within reach. There was a can in the car, underneath the driver's seat, at all times. There was a can of Pringles in the bedroom, in the kitchen, and, as I discovered one day when we ran out of toilet paper, in the bathroom, underneath the sink. No toilet paper, but plenty of potato chips. The fourth thing we consumed, because the mindless way we gorged could hardly be called eating, were TV dinners. Hungry Man dinners: Salisbury steak, fried chicken, baked fish, and cheese shells. Daddy bought us TV trays and, after Mommy left, we ate dinner on them almost exclusively.

My mother had her own food eccentricities. She hated pizza, insisting that the gooey white cheese and red tomato sauce looked like vomit. She also hated plums, insisting that they looked like breasts and it made her feel like a cannibal to bite into them. "Spoken like a true flat-chested woman," my father said, the first time Mommy confessed her reasoning. Later, it became a regular joke with him. My father eyed Mommy's small, dark, perfectly round breasts and would sing, in a sleepy Bing Crosby voice, "I'm in the mood for plums. Simply because you're near me." Mommy jumped up and ran, giggling, in the other direction until, finally, she let my father catch her and allowed him to kiss her neck, her mouth, and then the material that grazed her plumlike breasts.

♣

"Angela, you're going to be a star!" my father said, not caring that I was in the middle of not only dinner, but my show. His voice jingled with casino-coin promise.

He sat down on the bed next to me, dressed in a burgundy velour suit and a pink ruffled shirt. My feet dangled off the bed, ashy and gray. "Some star," I thought, looking down at my feet. Since my mother left, there was never enough lotion in the house. As many times as I reminded my father to buy more, he usually forgot. I'd taken to rubbing olive oil on my legs before I went outside, just so the kids on the street did not laugh at me.

I looked down at my father's feet; his shoes were a kind of dark cherry red. Shiny and unscuffed, they looked good enough to eat. I used to think that if my father loved me the way he loved his shoes, maybe I'd shine like that, too.

My father was meticulous about his wardrobe. Although he could care less about how filthy the toilet was or how many dirty dishes piled up in the sink, he washed and ironed his clothes religiously. Even when my mother was around, she wasn't allowed to touch his show clothes. The creases in his pants needed to be done just so. Shirts should fall on the hanger, like they were brand-new, just out of the box. Although it seemed like we were regularly short of money, my father found the cash to get his clothes dry-cleaned. Years later I learned my father bartered for almost everything he wore. He did magic shows for the Parks, who owned a cleaners on Thirty-fourth Street. He did bar mitzvahs for Maury, who sold him European shirts at wholesale prices, from a tiny shop on Rivington. He traded tricks for shoes with Enzo, the Italian shoemaker in the Village. Daddy even wrote a book about it, *Twentieth-Century Bartering: Mind Over Money*. Actually, it was more like a booklet. Twenty-two pages, single-spaced, perfectly bound by the copy shop that printed his head shot and resume.

"You're going to be a star!" Daddy repeated as I stared down at his shiny cherry shoes.

"Says who?" I asked, uninterested. My eyes drifted back to the television where Jimmy "J.J." Walker was getting into an argument with his television sister, Thelma. I'd developed an obsession with BernNadette Stanis, the actress who played Thelma, in the months since my mother left. I knew she was too young, but I wanted her to be my mother. I imagined that she'd come over to my house and show me stuff—like how to set my hair with sponge rollers and how to put on lipstick. At night, I dreamed she brought me lotion.

My father jumped up and snapped off the TV. "We're going to be on television. You and me together. It's a PBS telethon for the United Negro College Fund. It's a college thing, so they're only featuring teenage performers. So I told them you were fourteen—and that we are a father-daughter act."

My father couldn't easily shock me. I didn't know which bit of information to process first: that I was going to be on television, that I was going to perform with my father, or that he'd lied and told them I was fourteen. My twelfth birthday was still a few months away.

"No way is anyone going to believe that I'm fourteen," I started, my eyes darting to my nonexistent breasts.

My father's eyes followed mine and, for a moment, we both gazed at my chest and then, uncomfortable, looked away.

"Yeah, well, hmm," my father began. "There's stuff we can do to make you look older. Exercises and stuff."

My bottom lip fell again. Just a few weeks before, I'd read a Judy Blume novel where the main character, in a futile attempt to grow breasts, practiced this silly exercise while repeating, "I must. I must. I must increase my bust." I thought of my father, dressed in sweats like a gym teacher and blowing a whistle in my ear as I thrust my arms out and jutted them back in, repeating, "I must. I must. I must increase my bust." So many bad things happened to me that year. First, my mother disappeared. I'd seen some lady nearly die in the bathroom of Ecstasy. Then my father beat up Edward, my friend. But this was definitely the worst. Now I needed to grow breasts for my father, so we could be on television.

I got up, pretended to look out the window, and turned my back to my father. I grabbed the collar of my T-shirt and stared down at the place where my plums should be.

"When's the television show?" I asked, my back still turned.

"Soon," my father said. "We're going to have to start rehearsing every day. Thank God, it's summer and there's no school."

"Why? I know all of your tricks. I'll just hand you stuff."

My father put his arms on my shoulders and spun me around. "You've got to do more than hand me stuff, Angela!" he said, his voice thick with aggravation. "This is television. This is the big time. You're going to have to be a *real* assistant. We'll need new tricks and I'm going to have to make you disappear."

I'd never seen Mommy perform with my father. The few weeks, maybe months, when she worked as his assistant, I was never allowed to go to shows. Mommy did not tolerate me hanging out in nightclubs the way my father did. But I remembered her *Arabian Nights* outfit. I remembered her dancing lesson with the Indian woman. I remembered the word she'd used to explain why she couldn't do it. Was my father asking me to be his whore?

"What am I going to wear? A tuxedo?"

My father shook his head. "Not a tuxedo. No. I don't want you to look like a little boy."

I nodded, then excused myself. In the bathroom, after I brushed my teeth and while the door was still locked, I did the Judy Blume exercise. I silently repeated, "I must. I must. I must increase my bust." But when I woke up the next morning, my boobs had not grown even half an inch.

A few days later, my father took me to Manhattan to buy my assistant's costume. We took the car. I never saw my father take the subway or a bus in my life. If the car was in the shop, he hitched a ride with friends or he didn't go. I couldn't tell you if my father only cultivated friendships with men with wheels or if he was just good at hustling rides. I imagine he did a little of both. When we pulled up to Fifty-third Street, there was, of course, no parking. So my father did what he always did when he couldn't find a space: he double-parked. I hopped out; Daddy flashed the hazard lights and locked the door.

First, we went to a ballerina store called La Cerentola. All around me, there were black-and-white photos of thin, beautiful white women with sad, faraway looks in their eyes. The store was empty except for a very thin, dark-haired woman who wore a heavy cardigan over her leotard and leggings. She looked strange wearing that wool cardigan in the middle of the summer, like a bluebird wearing a muffler. She even fluttered when she walked, as if she had feathers.

"May I help you?" she asked in a nasal, heavily accented voice.

"I'm looking for a costume for my daughter," my father said, smiling, as if we hung out in weird white-girl shops all the time.

The woman turned on one leg, like a crane, and eyed me up and down. "You are a dancer?" She seemed insulted, as if my father said that I was the queen of England and she should curtsy.

I shook my head no and looked down at my legs. They were spindly and ashy and I regretted not oiling them before we left the house.

"I didn't think so!" she said. "Not with posture like that. Stand up straight, little girl."

I dropped my shoulders back and stuck out my nonexistent breasts.

"Better," she said, with a sniff.

My father seemed amused. "She's actually a magician's assistant. But I thought a dancer's costume might be a fun theme for the show. She's going to be on television."

The woman tilted her head and nodded, as if she understood. Wordlessly, she walked around the store and grabbed an armful of leotards and tutus. She called to me, *"Ma petite,"* and I followed her into the dressing room. Then she locked the door.

I shuddered and stepped back.

"These costumes are very expensive, eh. Very delicate and easy to tear. I will help you try them on. Take off your clothes."

I had never been naked in front of anyone except my mother. I stared at the ground as I peeled off my yellow T-shirt and undid my rainbow belt. I took off my denim shorts and shivered in my day of the week underwear. Not only were they holey, they weren't even the right day of the week.

The woman looked down at my rainbow socks and busted pink Converse sneakers. "The shoes. The socks. Take them off."

When I was done, she told me to sit down on a chair in the dressing room and reached for my foot. I wanted to cry at the sight of my dry black leg in her manicured white hand. She shimmied pink tights up one leg, then the other, and I felt like Cinderella trying on the glass shoe. For a moment, I wanted to kiss her. But instead, I stood and gazed at my legs in the full-length mirror. My ugly, ashy legs disappeared.

She handed me a pink leotard that was made of a soft, stretchy material. "You step into it, eh? Like so," she said, as she mimed the movement. Leotard and tights on, I stood taller and realized that I was almost as tall as the French bird woman. Maybe even almost as beautiful. I let out a breath and imagined myself, fourteen years old and on TV.

Then she held open the skirt of the tutu and helped me in. She snapped it behind me and opened the dressing room door. I stepped out of the musty dressing room and the air seemed to sweeten. My father was reading *Dance* magazine.

"What do you think?" I said, cupping my hands above my head and standing on my tippy toes like the ballerinas in the photos that surrounded me.

My father stuck out his tongue. "You look like a cotton candy machine exploded over you."

I put my arms down and stood feet flat. "I like it, Daddy," I begged. "Please let me wear it."

"You look ten, not fourteen," he said. Then turning to the saleswoman, he said, "I'll pick something out."

Two minutes later, there was a knock on the dressing room

door. My father's hand, brown, smooth fingers, reached into the musty box and handed me a pile of black satiny things. The saleswoman examined each garment: the fishnet stockings, the black V-neck leotard, the black satin miniskirt. Then she clucked her tongue and looked at me as if she was sorry I was my father's daughter.

There was no joy in dressing up in the clothes that Daddy selected. My legs created gray, ashy diamonds in the fishneck stockings. The black leotard hung from my shoulders like a funeral shroud. The satin miniskirt lifted from behind and you could almost see my booty.

"Now that's what I'm talking about!" my father said, as I walked out of the dressing room. Then he tossed me a black top hat and told me to put it on.

"Sophisticated lady!!!" he said, with a grin.

"Sir," the saleswoman said, jerking her head to the side. "May I have a word?"

The two of them stepped away and spoke in whispers so low, I could not hear them. I looked at myself in one of the store's mirrors and I wondered whether BernNadette Stanis ever wore an outfit like this, not on *Good Times* but if she did something like a Broadway play. I only wished the kids at school could see me, looking so grown-up.

If life with my father was a touring production of "Teddo, the Amazing Magician," then life with my mother was a kind of finishing school. I'd made my way through each stage, paying close attention to her expert tutelage. I understood our Saturday movie dates, the trips to the flea market and hairdresser to be a kind of schooling. It seemed that the costume my father chose for me was meant to continue my mother's lessons. This was what it meant to be a girl. Other girls at my school were more developed, more flirtatious, but I was convinced that I was the only girl in the sixth grade who went to nightclubs, who drank vodka and orange juice, who was going to be on TV.

My father returned with the saleswoman. He was all smiles, but her thin lips were pressed too tightly together for her to actually look pleased.

"Let's take it off and wrap it up, *chérie*," she said. And so we did.

♣

My father took me to Bloomingdale's to buy a bra. Only one girl in the entire sixth grade wore a bra: Brandi Freeman. The rowdy boys in the cafeteria ran up behind her and took turns snapping it. For reasons I could never understand, they thought this was the funniest thing in the world. They'd fall down on the floor laughing, then pick themselves up and do it again. As the escalator climbed to the fourth floor, "Foundations," I thanked God I was never going to wear a bra to school.

My father walked through the aisles of bras and panties like he was Shaft out on a stroll. As I watched the grown women around me, I felt embarrassed to be in such a place with my father, of all people. As their eyes brushed past us, I wondered if they thought my father regularly saw me in my underwear.

We passed several white saleswomen, but my father didn't speak until we saw a black one. She was beautiful: chocolate brown, legs for days, with a cap of black curls that hung luxuriously from her head. She smiled at my father through her glossy scarlet lips. Then she smiled at me.

"How can I help you today?" she asked.

"I need to buy my daughter a bra," my father said, gesturing at my flat chest.

"Hmmm," she said, sizing me up; then, "Follow me." We followed her as her long legs galloped around the circular racks. "We do have some preteen bras." She gestured to a display of bralettes: pastel-colored undershirts cut into a bra-style shape.

My father shook his head. "I'm looking for something to fill her out a little."

He took the costume out of the bag and showed her. "She needs something to wear under this."

The woman looked me up and down, then looked at the costume. "It's a little early for Halloween, honey," she said, slipping into homegirl mode.

"It's not for Halloween, sugar," my father said, sweet-talking her right back. "My little girl's going to be on television."

"Well, she looks a little young for that outfit," she said, in a tone that suggested she might like to try it on herself.

"She's a lot older than she looks," my father said. "She's going to be fifteen in a few months."

"Yeah right," said the saleswoman, giving me a wicked grin. "And I just celebrated my twenty-first birthday."

I watched my father and the saleswoman eye each other hungrily and in my head, repeated a line I'd seen on TV: "Get a room. Get a room."

"Happy birthday, baby," my father said, continuing to flirt, outrightly devilish now. "I'm really sorry I didn't get to taste any of your cake."

The woman yelped as if my father had reached out and tickled the back of her knee. She grinned, then snapped and turned on her heels. "You are trouble," she said, waving a finger at my father. "Come with me, little girl. Bring your Halloween costume with you."

She held my hand as we rounded the store. At the dressing room, she handed me a stack of 32-AA padded bras and told me to try them on.

I took the dance shop costume and the bras and locked the door to the dressing room. As I took my clothes off, I could hear Teddo and the saleswoman flirting.

"Sho, you're right," I heard her giggle.

"You got a license for that?" I heard him whisper.

I laced the bra over my shoulders and struggled to hook it behind me. I snapped my elbows backward and wrestled with the material until my arms were sore. It seemed like I'd been in the sweaty dressing room forever, but my father didn't notice.

"Excuse me," I said through the closed door. They kept talking.

"Excuse me," I said, a little louder, pressing my lips to the crack in the door.

"So what's your number?" my father said.

"Do you really think I want you to ring my bell, sweetheart?" the saleswoman answered.

"I need some help!" I finally yelled as loud as I could.

The dressing room door shook. "What's going on in there?" the saleswoman asked. Her voiced sounded worried.

I cracked the door, pulled her in, and closed it quickly behind her. "I can't close it," I said, in my sweetest voice.

"That's because you're putting it on wrong," she said. She took the bra off, turned it face front, held the hook underneath my tiny breast, then slid it back around and guided my arms through. It was like watching someone do a dance so elaborate you knew you could never repeat it.

"Your first bra and your mama's missing a moment like this?" the woman asked, straightening out the straps.

"She'd be here, but she's dead," I said, in my best Orphan Annie voice. I looked down, then looked at her from the very top of my eyelids like I'd seen Tatum O'Neal do in *Paper Moon*.

She wrapped her arms around me and held me tight. "That's just too bad, sugar. But remember, God doesn't give you nothing you can't handle. I bet your mama's looking down on you from heaven and she's really proud."

"Do you really think so?" I said as I wriggled into the fishnets then stepped into the black leotard and satin skirt.

"I really think so," she said, opening the dressing room door.

There was no mirror in the dressing room so I didn't see myself until I was standing in front of my father. My hair was knotty but my face was still the same—dark like my mother's, same nose, same full lips. But from the neck down, I looked different. The bra gave the illusion of cleavage and the cleavage gave me the illusion of hips.

"Not bad, not bad," my father said. Then turning to the saleswoman, he said, "How about you hook her up with a little makeup? She's going to need makeup to be on TV."

The woman went to the counter for her purse then sat me down in the dressing room. She brushed green stuff on my eyes, poked me with a black liner pencil, battered my cheeks like they were two chickens ready for the fryer, and then colored my lips. I'd never worn lipstick before and it felt thick and sludgy, like I'd been eating mud pie.

"She looks hot," the saleswoman said, admiring her handiwork. "What kind of show is she going to be on?"

"A telethon. United Negro College Fund."

"Well, that face and that tight little body are going to make those college boys some money," the saleswoman said, winking at my father.

I stepped up to the mirror, half afraid that the bad-ass girl who was staring me down was going to pop me one if I dared get too close. It wasn't Mommy's style. I looked more like Lola Falana than Cleopatra Jones. But Mommy wasn't around and I liked it. I liked feeling so pretty, so hot stuff, so not me.

"What about shoes?" I asked my father, looking down at my stockinged feet.

"We'll get those later," he said, his eyes never leaving the saleswoman's pretty face.

I was ready to go home. New shoes were coming and I was willing to bet, dollars to doughnuts, that they were going to be high heels.

♣

The box where my father made me disappear was shaped to look like a nineteenth-century dollhouse, a grand Greek Revival with a dozen opaque windows, a tiny wooden door, and stately Doric columns. It smelled of cherrywood and the name of the wood made me think of George Washington. I counted each of my cues by the seconds, and the time I spent "disappeared" seemed endless. My father took my hand like a scene out of *My Fair Lady* and led me up to the dollhouse's matching footstool. I climbed into the dollhouse taking care not to slip. No small feat in my first pair of heels.

In our living room, I stood to face an imaginary audience, lifting both hands into the air, gracefully, like a Rockette. Then I knelt on my knees as my father latched the dollhouse all around me. Inside: not more than two feet in any direction, total darkness and, of course, silence. My job was to slip open the trapdoor, climb into the dollhouse's base, and monitor my breath so I did not hyperventilate while my father took four square flat blades and inserted them into the strategic openings in the dollhouse's facade.

We practiced the swords in the dollhouse trick for hours a day, every day, for three weeks. Even with a dull blade, the knife closest to my hand eventually drew blood. I kept expecting it, but still I was startled, as if I'd been sucker-punched by a known enemy while I was stupidly looking the other way. I remembered Mommy and the calamity with the scarves and I did not cry out. I put the cut on my hand to my lips and sucked silently. Then I smudged the bleeding spot into the secret trapdoor. I could never tell my father what he did to me, all the ways in which living with him was like living in a house of mirrors and knives.

"Stop fidgeting!" my father yelled, when my movement shook the box ever so slightly. "You're supposed to have disappeared. We're not playing goddamn hide and seek."

"I'm sorry," I whispered, wondering what it looked like, on the outside, to see a dollhouse talking.

"Sorry didn't do it, you did!" my father continued, and I could hear the weight of his feet cutting into the rug. "It's like you're a two-year-old! Don't you want to be on TV?"

"Fuck you," I thought, summoning the rage I once watched Mommy explode with but could never feel. "Fuck you," I mouthed the words in the dark place where I hid, for hours it seemed, all so my father could be famous. In the dark, those kind of words felt good.

When he let me out, I didn't dare repeat what I said inside. I glared and pouted until he got the point. But that was the thing about my father: he was so in love with himself, so thoroughly fastened to his worldview, that it took a lot for him to notice he'd done something wrong. And it took a whole lot more than that for him to care. Which is why even when I showed him my bleeding hand, he was all smiles.

"That's what Band-Aids are made for, right, princess?" He grabbed me and swung me in the air. "We're going to be famous! Big things are going to happen. You watch. Your mother's going to be sorry she left us."

I nodded, agreeing. I did not want to spite my mommy, but I hoped that my mommy would see us on TV and be sorry. As I went in search of a Band-Aid, I let myself believe that a reminder to be sorry was all Mommy needed to come on home.

♣

The day my father and I appeared, for the very first time, on television was something like Christmas. The joy was in the waking. An hour before I heard the bleating of my father's alarm clock, I lay in bed, eyes open and legs curled into my chest as if I was waiting to be born. I knew the drill because we'd practiced it like a pregnant woman rehearsing the way to the hospital. My father woke up at five. He showered first then he woke me up. While I was in the shower, he made breakfast. Omelets, which we ate in the car on paper plates. At seven, we left for Funeka's apartment in Queens. Funeka was the saleswoman we met in Bloomingdale's. Her sister did hair and Funeka was going to do my makeup and help me get dressed. It all went according to plan, until I sat in the basement of Funeka's house. At the first smell of the burning hot comb, I began to cry.

"Don't cry, sugar," Funeka's sister, Layla, cooed at me. Her hair was straight and long, in contrast to Funeka's pixieish cut, but their bodies were the same: so narrow and lean that I imagined they might bend perfectly in half, the top part disappearing into a sliver in the bottom, like a pocket knife. "I haven't even touched you yet," she said.

I was not afraid, although this was the first time my hair was straightened. I was sorry that I did not ask what Layla was going to do to my hair. The first time my hair was straightened should have been with my grandmother's hot comb.

I began to cry then and nervously wiped my eyes.

"It's not going to burn, baby."

"I'm okay," I told Layla. "I was just thinking about my mother."

Layla squeezed my shoulder. "You take all the time you need, dear heart. Funeka told me all about it. You take all the time you need." My father said that my mother wasn't dead, but it was already August and she had been gone for a long time. I hadn't heard a word from her. If she wasn't dead, I needed her to be. I practiced all the rituals of loss I'd ever seen on TV or read about in a book because saying good-bye was the best I could do. I did not know how to love her living, if living away from me was what she was going to do.

♣

By ten o'clock that morning we were at the studio, a warehouse of a building on the far west side of Manhattan. We parked the car and quickly learned all the things that my father was wrong about when he described our television debut. One, there was no red carpet, no paparazzi, no hordes of screaming fans pushed back behind a royal blue police barricade outside. The address on our letter led us to a generic glass door, where we spoke to a bored security guard who barely opened his sleepy eyes to check us off on a list of approved guests and point us in the right direction. Two, there was no dressing room. When my father asked about one, the station manager, a charming black man who reminded me of Gordon Robinson on *Sesame Street*, laughed out loud. "Now, that's a good one, my Houdini-like brother," he said, clapping Daddy on the shoulder and leading us to the green room where we were to wait with all the other guests. Another thing: the green room was not really green; the walls were a kind of pinkish orange color, like the color of your tongue after you've spent all day eating Now and Laters.

After two hours in the green room, we met our first bonafide star. She was beautiful. She was wearing an off-the-shoulder blue sequined gown. Her skin was the color of sun tea and her hair fell in soft waves around her face, like she was a black Barbie. She was Miss Black America. We knew this because she wore a sash, just like the Miss Americas on TV. It said in blue sequined letters: "Miss Black America." Her name was Ethiopia Brown and she was hosting the telethon. Gordon, the station manager, brought her right over to Daddy and me and she shook our hands.

"So pleased to meet you," she said, in a voice that was airy and rich like a Milky Way bar. "The United Negro College Fund is helping to send me to college, so this is a cause very dear to my heart."

"How long have you been Miss Black America?" I asked.

"For almost a year now, honey," she said, reaching out to squeeze my hand. "It's been great. Next month, in Kansas City, I'm going to have to relinquish my crown, but it's been amazing. I've met all kinds of wonderful people. I spent four weeks in Europe, singing for the troops at the USO. I even got to guest star in an episode of *Fantasy Island*."

"No way!" I asked, struggling to remember what episode she was on. "Who did you play?"

"Just a small part, just a contestant in a beauty pageant. But I also did a movie: I had three lines in the sequel to *Roots*."

My father's ears perked up. "Now that is something."

The station manager tapped Miss Black America on the shoulder. "Ethiopia, you're back up in five."

I knew I didn't have a lot of time, but I couldn't ask her the question I'd been wanting to ask since she walked into the green room, the blue sequins on her sash sparkling so bright. Turns out I didn't need to. She stood up to leave, shook Daddy's hand, and then knelt down to whisper in my ear. "You can do it. You could be Miss Black America. Remember, poise is everything."

Then she gave me a little hug and headed out the door.

I didn't know what that word meant, "poise." But I promised myself I'd look it up the minute I got home.

Daddy squeezed my shoulder. "What did she whisper to you?" he asked, smiling as if it must have something to do with him.

"Nothing."

"Didn't look like nothing."

"It's a secret," I said, staring down at my fishnet legs.

"Fair enough," Daddy said, shrugging and reaching for a magazine. "You've got yours and I've got mine."

I smelled the bait and wanted to bite, but let it go.

♣

At four o'clock, Daddy and I went into the main studio to set up for our act. The stage was tiny. Crowds of people answering telephones that we'd seen on the television in the green room were, in fact, not crowds at all. There were sixteen people, eight on either side of the stage. There were three cameras and Daddy said that while the lights were hot, the studio was freezing, the air-conditioning turned up full blast. "You have to keep the cameras cool," he explained. "That's some expensive equipment." Miss Black America stood off to the side watching the performer, a foul-mouthed young comedian dressed in drag. "He's no Geraldine," my father said dismissively. I nodded in agreement. Flip Wilson was a god in our house.

The emcee announced our act and Daddy whispered to me, "Keep on smiling, Angela. No matter what. Pretend that the cameras aren't there and you're having the best time of your life." Which is what I did. We ran through the dollhouse trick without a nick or a miss. When I disappeared, I could actually hear Miss Black America gasp. And when Daddy took all the knives out of the dollhouse, spinning it around, once, twice, and then a third time, my heart pounded against the secret trapdoor. When Daddy opened the dollhouse to reveal that I was actually there, I could feel the camera taking me in—my freshly straightened hair, my Flori Roberts lips, the rounded shape of my padded bra, the satin skirt swishing around my hips, the fishnet stockings, my legs, glistening with Vaseline underneath, and my black, shiny, leather pumps, one inch high. I bowed and gave the camera my best Kool-Aid grin.

Finally, I understood why my father wanted so bad to be famous. You spend your whole life trying not to disappear. Your mother and father fight, and a little of you disappears. You go to the first day of school in last year's clothes and a little of you disappears. There's not even enough money for TV dinners, so you eat eggs, three times a day, for three days in a row, and the next time your father cracks an egg and throws the shell away, he's also throwing away a little bit of you, the part that feels strong enough to face the world. Your mother is gone, taking your heart with her, but that's not all. Every time you look at her picture, every time you wish she was there, it's like her ghost has come back to pinch off a little more. Not heart, because you don't have any to give away. Just the sliver that belongs to your father and the rusty heart socket that enables you to live. She wants skin. So you scrape the inside of your thigh with your father's razor and you give it to her. You used to love her. You used to worship her. But now she's a cowboy who's changed sides and every time you try to remember her, it's a showdown between the angel who was your mother and the wanted-poster desperado who's taken her place.

You look at your mother's picture, the one with the baby who isn't you, and you look at your sweet, fucked-up father and you wonder who's worse. The one who left or the one who stayed behind to screw up, again and again and again. It's a gunfight. The desperado wins. She always does and when she walks off into the sunset, a round red piece of you slides around in her pocket, like a marble. Not satisfied, she comes back to cut a lock of your hair, to nibble your nails, to knock a tooth out of the back of your mouth where no one sees it, and the empty cavity becomes a hole where you go to call up memory. You fight every day against disappearing and being on TV makes you whole, more than whole; it beams you out to a million electric boxes where you live in bright, all-temperature Tide colors. In that magic box, you are happy; everything is perfect and you are safe.

♣

Back in the green room, Daddy was doing card tricks and I was still grinning, my smile wide over a cold can of Coca-Cola. The station manager came in and asked to speak to my father. My father stepped out and came back, ecstatic. "Angela, honey," he said, "let's go."

In the car, he told me that not only did the station get 150 pledges in the ten minutes after our act, the highest record for the day, but they also received a call. Muhammad Ali, or rather a man who works for Muhammad Ali, saw the program. Did my father know that the champ is also an amateur magician? Did my father want to meet the greatest boxer who ever lived?

"I'm going to meet him tonight," Daddy said. "But first, we're going to celebrate." Daddy took me to Harlem for dinner; Sammy and Uncle Roger met us there. Afterward, he told Sammy to take me home. He and Roger were going to meet Ali. He kissed me on the forehead and then, like the magician he was, my father was gone.

♣

Driving in my father's car, Sammy smiled handsomely, next to me. I almost felt like I was on a date. My mother once said I needed to be at least sixteen to date, but my mother wasn't around and my father was serving up a new deal.

"I like your stockings," Sammy said.

"Thanks."

"Dig those shoes."

"Thanks."

"Never seen a satin skirt so shiny!"

"Sammy, come on!" I said, embarrassed. "It's just me."

"Hmmm, we'll see about that."

♣

Back at the apartment, Sammy kept making me nervous.

"Where's your room?" he asked.

"You know where it is, Sammy," I said, clinging to the far arm of the couch.

"Let's go see it. You got any games? Let's play Twister."

"I don't have any games," I told him. "You don't have to stay. My father leaves me alone all the time. I'm old enough. I don't need a sitter."

"I don't mind. Ain't got nothing else to do. Wonder what your father's doing right now. Probably having a drink with Muhammad Ali. The greatest. Man, your dad knows how to make friends and influence people. Goddamn! Muhammad Ali."

"Do you think Ali knows BernNadette Stanis?"

"Who?"

"You know, she plays Thelma on *Good Times*. I want to meet her one day. Maybe if things go well tonight with Ali, he might be able to introduce me."

"Child, please," Sammy said. "Ali ain't got nothing to do with no Thelma on no *Good Times*. That girl would be lucky to clean his shoes."

I looked away.

"I guess I should put on my pajamas and get to bed."

"Okay, I'll come tuck you in."

"You don't have to."

"Well, I'd like to."

I shrugged and went into my room. Just hours before, I was on TV, looking like a grown woman, making friends with Miss Black America. Now Sammy wanted to treat me like I was a little girl.

♣

I changed into my pajamas, summer ones with a sleeveless top and purple flowers. Then I crawled underneath the covers. Sammy sat at the edge of the bed.

"It's been a long time since I tucked a girl into bed, Angela."

He kissed me on the mouth and I froze. He worked his way down my neck with his tongue, while his hand traveled up my pajama top. I wore the padded bra to bed. I told myself it was because the bra felt good, but part of me knew that I wore it because I knew Sammy might do exactly what he was doing.

He unhooked the strap expertly and eased the pajama top over my head. His eyes were closed and his lips traveled leisurely from my neck down to my nipples and when he reached that small, dark, raised spot, we both jumped. Me because the feeling of his tongue was so electric and delicious that I was sure I was about to die. When I recovered, I looked over at Sammy, to encourage him to continue, when I saw that he was crying.

"They're so little. There's nothing there at all," he sobbed, silently. "You're just a little girl."

I put my arms around him, the way I saw my mother do sometimes when my father had no bookings for weeks and he was too broke for braggadocio. I laid his head on my chest as he kept repeating the same line again and again. "You're so little. You're so little."

"I know, honey," I said, imagining that I was BernNadette Stanis on *Good Times*, giving my man the love and support he needed. "I know."

We lay on the bed for a few minutes and I thought maybe we'd try again, maybe Sammy would start it up again. Good lovin' was what the kids used to call it, as in "Lisa cut school and went to the hooky house. Jerome gave her some of that good lovin'." Before, I did not know what it meant. I didn't think any of the kids in my sixth-grade class were actually having sex, so I figured it was something else. Now I knew. Good lovin' was when a boy put his hands or his tongue someplace he wasn't supposed to and it felt so good, you nearly said your name backward. I was hoping for a little more, but I was out of luck. Sammy rolled me over and gently closed each of the three clasps on my preteen bra. He was deliberate and careful, like a master chef putting away his favorite set of ironclad pots. He paused for a second; I could feel his fingers rest on the small of my back and I know he heard it too, the door between us slamming shut. Then I felt his fingers again, tucking in the tag of the bralette underneath the narrow expanse of satiny purple that spanned my back.

I turned again, lying face up, and he sat on the bed beside me.

"Your father's going to kill me," Sammy said. The fear in his voice made his words sound thick and slow.

I thought then of his tongue on my nipple, watering my plum, and how he'd made it grow and how Edward got his ass kicked just for thinking about the kinds of things Sammy did. My father would kill Sammy if he knew, but I wasn't telling. "He'll never know, sugar," I said, letting the grown woman words ooze out of my mouth like honey out of a jar. "He'll never know."

He held my hand and we sat there, in the dark, in silence. It was all so dizzying, the sweetness of him squeezing my hand; the pulsing place between my legs; the fear that we'd be caught coupled with the unspeakable boldness of not caring; and the memory of the moment when Sammy's shame demanded payment and his tears began to run down my chest. I wanted to keep each thing separate, his lips and his tears, bottle up the kisses and call it love, but they swirled together like a palm full of dirt and spit; I couldn't shake the dirt off my hand even if I tried.

♣

Once, I was standing on a subway platform with Mommy at a station that stood four tracks deep. We were waiting for the local and there was no one around but us and an old white man, who was sitting so far down the platform, I couldn't see if he was reading the *Daily News* or the *New York Post.* Mommy and I were laughing and joking. "I'm a widow from the South Side!" she said. I was just about to repeat my line, when the local train on the other side arrived with a thunderous rumble. Then the express trains rocketed by on the middle tracks and there was so much wind, Mommy held me back from the edge. By the time our train arrived, all screeches and roars, I could hardly remember the waiting, its deadly quiet, the hollowness of the station minutes before.

That night after Sammy left, I lay awake trying to make sense of how quickly my world changed. My mother left and my heart was empty like that station. Mommy disappeared, a magic trick. Then Sammy gave me a taste of his good lovin' and I could barely stand for the wind.

Of Course It's Hot in Africa

We did not

see Sammy again that summer. I looked for him every time I stepped into a nightclub, every time Uncle Roger pulled up in front of our house. But he was a ghost. Daddy and Uncle Roger did not think his absence was strange, but they seemed to enjoy coming up with theories to explain where he might be. "Sammy must've found himself a woman," Daddy said one afternoon. We were having lunch at Lalibela's, the Ethiopian restaurant where Gigi, Uncle Roger's new girlfriend, worked. We ate chicken wat, with *injera*, pieces of purply white flatbread, while Gigi flitted by between orders to kiss Uncle Roger on his forehead. We'd only been to Lalibela's a few times, but I was developing a serious passion for Ethiopian food and the pure pleasure of no forks, no knives, just using our hands and the *injera* to scoop the food into our mouths.

"Maybe he went to visit his sister in Michigan," Uncle Roger said.

"Sister?" my father said. "I didn't know he had a sister." My father made a face. "Ooo, wonder if she's got those thick glasses and that big Lionel Ritchie forehead."

They went on like that for a few minutes, making off-color jokes about how ugly Sammy's sister must be and how in the dark, pussy don't have no color. I wondered if that's what Sammy thought about me. In the dark, did it not matter that I was only eleven years old? In the dark was I as beautiful, as desirable, as Miss Black America?

♥

A few weeks before school began, I met Muhammad Ali after a sparring match in Atlantic City. I'd never been to the Jersey Shore and as we drove, I was more interested in the beach and the boardwalk than in Daddy's boxing match. I knew that Muhammad Ali was famous and that Daddy getting to meet him after the telethon was a huge deal. But I didn't really care about athletes. "Come on. We're going to miss the whole thing," Daddy said, dragging me from a novelty shop that sold the Atlantic City skyline in snowglobes, black-and-white postcards of 1920s bathing beauties in old-fashioned swimsuits, and other memorabilia.

I tugged in the other direction. "I'm hungry. Will you buy me some lunch?"

"Later!" Daddy said, tugging back.

"How about some saltwater taffy?" I asked, as Daddy speed-walked down the boardwalk.

"How about you give me a break, Angela?"

"Will there be any famous people there?" I asked as we raced down the block toward the boxing gym.

"Angela, did you not hear me say that we are going to see Muhammad Ali?"

"I know he's going to be there," I said. "Will there be anybody else?"

"Anybody else like who?" my father asked, losing all patience with me.

"BernNadette Stanis?" I asked. My father ignored me.

"How about Melba Moore?"

Silence.

"Phyllis Hyman?"

♥

After the fight, my father grabbed my hand and led me through a tunnel of men who smelled of smoke and alcohol, even at four in the afternoon. Daddy got the nod from one bodyguard, then the other, and each approval took us into a room filled with fewer and fewer people. Until finally we were in a plushly decorated living room. Four long-legged Diana Ross look-alikes in fancy off-the-shoulder dresses and feathered hair were draped across a couch. Each woman had the sensual pout and slightly bored expression of a sultan's odalisque. There were groups of three or four men gathered in each corner. My father walked over to a group of men in the far corner and made easy conversation. One guy slapped Daddy on the back and another shook his hand, just a few seconds too long. Men liked my father, his charm and trickery.

When one guy asked me, "How do you like the fights, little girl?" I played along, proud to be my father's assistant: part doll girl, part circus monkey, all wonderful. I rolled up my sleeve, flexed an invisible muscle, and growled, "I *love* a good fight." This got a big laugh and my father looked pleased.

In deep plush armchairs closest to Ali's private room, what seemed to be the three wise men guarded the barn door. I never knew how legendary the knights were that sat at Ali's roundtable. I remembered them only by the secret names I gave them: the man with the scary hair, Witch Head; the man who told a million jokes, Mighty Mouth; and the man with the camera, Flash Gordon.

When Ali emerged, he greeted his handlers first, then moved through each circle in the room, shaking hands and making proclamations. When he got to my father, his grin seemed to broaden. "The Magic Man!" he said. "When you going to start teaching me some tricks?"

My father glowed with bright wattage. You could see he felt anointed. "You just tell me when, Muhammad," he said. "I want you to meet my daughter, Angela. Angela Davis Brown."

Ali took me in his arms and I was in love. He kissed me on the cheek and said only one word, "Princess."

Ali was wearing a robe and was clearly not showered. I could feel the sweat of his skin dampen my thin T-shirt. All that I saw before—the pummeling, the brutality and arrogance of what took place in the ring—was forgotten. Here was a man, perhaps the greatest man, picking me up as if I was a doll. I did not know what to do beyond the moment of our embrace, but I desperately wished for it not to end. I wanted all these people to go away and leave me with Ali. I wanted to whisper in his ear the words of an old Dinah Washington song my father often played. "Teach me tonight," I wanted to sing. But I was punch-drunk and said nothing.

My father pressed into the gap. "I could teach you a few tricks, Muhammad," he said. "You can float like a butterfly in the ring. But I can teach you how to stand on thin air."

Then my father turned and walked away. At the door frame, he paused. He turned, smiled, and when he turned again, he appeared not to move forward but up. He floated there for a few moments, then, like a bird, gently rested on the ground again.

Ali was pleased. "I like that," he said, rubbing his chin with a curious gaze. "Talk to Angelo, man. Come up and see me."

Ali called out to one of the triumvirate of wise men sitting at his door. "Hey, Angelo," he said. "Hook me up with the magic man."

That night I had a dream that I've had a hundred times since. Mommy and Daddy are in a boxing ring. Dressed in electric-colored shorts, they scowl at each other from their corners. In the dream, my father is bare-chested and Mommy wears a white man's undershirt. But depending on the night, the color of their shorts changes. Sometimes Mommy is in bright red and my father is wearing blue. Sometimes she wears yellow and he wears green.

The action, however, never changes. When the bell rings, Mommy gets the first shot in, nailing my father with a strong right hook. But she is soon worn down; my father hits harder, he hits faster. But he does not win. My father's arms are thrown around Mommy's neck. She drags him this way and that, all around the ring. I don't know if they are dancing, but I hear music. I see myself standing at the judges' table and I am singing. They fight, they dance, and I sing.

♥

After our trip to Atlantic City, my father was invited to Ali's training camp in Deer Park, Pennsylvania. The ride down was like four hours in a two-seater sauna. Daddy's ancient Mercedes' air conditioner was broken and the weather outside was hitting 100 degrees. His mechanic offered him a loaner car, but my father wanted to show up at the training camp in the Mercedes.

"You should have taken the loaner," I said, sticking my head out of the window. The air wasn't cool, but at least on the New Jersey Turnpike we were going fast enough to feel a little breeze.

"Show up to meet Muhammad Ali in some loaner beater? I don't think so," my father fumed.

I tugged at the daishiki my father made me wear. "And nobody, I mean nobody, wears these anymore. It's 1980, not 1970, Daddy."

"We are going to spend a week with one of the greatest black men to ever walk this earth and all you do is complain!" My father rolled up his window, then made me do the same to mine.

"Can I open the window, Daddy, please?" I pleaded ten minutes later.

He glared at me; beads of sweat had formed around his brow and his hair seemed to be sinking under the weight of the humidity. "How many times do I have to tell you," he said. "You can't open the window because I have the air on."

I rolled my eyes and looked away. Now my father was going to pretend that the air-conditioning was working, one of his favorite torture techniques. He didn't consider it lying, more like a deep conviction in things that weren't true.

"The air doesn't work, Daddy," I muttered, my mouth twisted to the side in disgust.

"Sure it does!" Daddy said cheerily, putting his hand out to an open vent. "Matter of fact, I should turn the air down 'cause it's eating up all of my gas."

I tried another tactic.

"Why don't they make these with short sleeves?" I asked, tugging at my daishiki. "Isn't it hot in Africa?"

"Of course it's hot in Africa," said my father, who was dressed in a white cotton long-sleeved shirt, a navy blue tie with a colorful image of Africa on it, and navy blue slacks. His jacket was carefully spread out across the backseat.

"That daishiki is designed to keep you cool."

I looked at the sweat marks creeping out from underneath each arm then bent down to sniff myself. It hadn't even been two hours since we left Brooklyn and I was straight-up funkafied.

"I stink," I moaned, peering out the window at the miles of traffic. "Are we there yet?"

♥

I did not know that summer, when we met the king of the world, that Ali was a great boxer in decline. I was too young to know anything about Cassius Clay, Sonny Liston, his relationship with Malcolm X and the Nation of Islam, or the Rumble in the Jungle. My father must have known, but he did not care. Ali was training for a comeback. He was going to fight a title bout with Larry Holmes and, as Drew Bundini Brown so famously proclaimed in Zaire, "The king was coming home for his throne." The fight, however, was still months away, which meant there was time for Daddy to teach the king a little magic.

At the camp, my father learned quickly that even in relative down periods, everybody wanted a piece of the champ's attention, so he concentrated on tricks that could be done in a matter of seconds. Daddy took a card and put it between Ali's monster-sized mitts. He shuffled through the deck until he found Ali's card. He separated Ali's hands and miraculously, the card Ali squeezed so tightly was a different card. Then he asked Ali to choose a card. Daddy threw the whole deck in the air and when the cards came fluttering down, only one card, Ali's card, was stuck to the ceiling.

♥

Daddy and I slept in a small cabin that was one of more than a dozen guest houses that dotted the camp. The sparring partners slept in bunk beds in one big house. Ali had built a house for his family and a house where he slept alone when a big fight was only weeks away. There was another small cabin designated as a mosque. Ali prayed five times a day there.

There were horses at the camp and five stables. Every day, the horse's trainer gave me riding lessons on a pony. After just a few days, I was beginning to get it, to love the feeling of the pony underneath me, being swept along by the pony's strength and speed. For the first time I understood why Daddy spoke so admiringly about a great car having horsepower. The trainer walked the pony down a long trail and my father sat on a rock and watched. He was motionless and smiling until I couldn't see him anymore. But when we returned, he was there, in the same position, as still as a Buddha. Being at the camp of the most well-known black man in the world did not relax my father's dress code any. Yes, it was August, but he still wore a suit every day. The only concession he made to the casual nature of the camp was an unbuttoned shirt and the occasional safari suit.

"I like to see you riding horses," he said to me one night in the cabin before turning out the lights. There were two twin beds in our room with a night table between us. I liked it. Spending the nights there with Daddy, I imagined, was like going to sleep-away camp the way other girls in my school did.

"It's not really a horse, it's a pony. And I'm not really riding yet. Mr. Widdicombe is just pulling me along."

"All of the things I've seen you do, perform on TV, play lacrosse, ride horses," my father said, ignoring me. "Your mother and I always wanted you to have these kinds of opportunities."

I turned onto my side and shook my head. "Daddy, you've never seen me play lacrosse."

He tapped his head. "I can imagine it, though. When I saw that black girl at that school running around with that funny stick, I knew you could do it too. She was just as good as any of those white girls."

"Sarah," I said, letting her name drop like a coin in a wishing fountain.

My father jumped up and began doing his smoker's pace. "Look where we are, baby! Look where we are. We're hanging out with Muhammad Ali."

"I know, Daddy."

Daddy's stockinged feet sounded like a soft-shoe, crossing back and forth along the hardwood floors of the cabin. There was joy in his step, but sadness too. "Your mother left us to be a movie star," he said, shuffling along, like he was a long-lost member of the Nicholas Brothers. "But we're the stars, Angela. *We're* the stars."

He came over to my bed and kissed me on the cheek, but my father fell asleep first that night. I watched his face in the moonlight, the paleness of his skin, the dark stubble on his cheek, the soft curly hair that was more Euro than Afro. When Mommy left, I got to know my father from all angles. I began to gauge the measure of the man. I wanted Mommy to have stayed, to have taught me about menstruation and lipstick and the way my body was changing. I wanted her to take me to movies, to curl my eyelashes, to be a bad mamajama. My father could never have done those things and he never did. But as I got older, I began to gauge the measure of him and this gave me a measure of who I might be. My father always told me he wanted to give me the world and there at Ali's training camp he started to make good on his promise.

I did not have my art kit, but I'd brought along my pencils and a pad. As Daddy slept, I drew another comic. In the first panel, there was a picture of me at school. The lettering read:

♥♥♥

BY DAY, THE MILD MANNERED ANGELA DAVIS BROWN
IS A REGULAR 6TH GRADER.

♥♥♥

In the second panel, I drew a picture of me in a Batgirl costume and the lettering read:

♥♥♥

A WARD OF THE COURT SINCE HER MOTHER
MYSTERIOUSLY DISAPPEARED, SHE PROWLS
THE STREET AT NIGHT, AS BATGIRL . . .

♥♥♥

In the third panel, I drew a picture of me and Teddo sleeping upside down. He wore a top hat and I was in my Batgirl costume. It read:

♥♥♥

DURING THE DAY, SHE AND HER FATHER,
THE MAGIC MAN, SLEEP IN HER BATCAVE.

♥♥♥

The next day, Daddy took me to afternoon training. He told me that Ali's big fight was against a man who was once one of his sparring partners. "You never know," Daddy whispered, "just where people will end up. The man who's serving you hot dogs today could be the president of the company you want to work for next week."

Training stopped when an old man appeared at the door. He had skin the color of ginger and he shuffled up to the ring in an immaculate beige linen shirt, black pants with knife-sharp pleats, cracked but polished leather shoes, and almost unbelievably, a green trucker's cap.

"Ali, meet José Antonio," said the trainer who stood at the old man's elbow. "He's ninety-four years old."

"Ninety-four!" Ali said. "I can't believe it."

He took his gloves off and jumped out of the ring.

"What have you been eating, old man?"

The old man grinned. "A lot of women."

♥

That night, after dinner, Mr. Widdicombe took a bunch of us out on a hay ride. Ali owned an old circus cart and Mr. Widdicombe hitched it up to four horses. He sat in the front and we all sat in the back on the U-shaped bench that wrapped around three edges of the cart. I didn't know any of the men. I was the only girl and the only kid. The guys all called me "princess," the way Ali did, and I took it as a compliment. Later, in more cynical moments, I wondered if the nickname only saved them the trouble of learning and remembering my name.

Once they greeted me, their conversation turned to the world of men and it seemed that, perhaps, boxing was a microcosm of politics and nations, princes and kings. They talked about Ali's comeback, about how he looked in the ring, whether he had any joy in his swing, and whether he still showed enough bounce in his toes. They talked about someone called Holmes and how much they missed a man named Pacheco. They talked about the president and the corporate CEOs who flew private jets to Vegas bouts and how, no matter what, the mob got their cut.

They described a universe as complicated as a chess game, and even if I could keep all the names straight, I could not figure out how these pieces moved. Was it the liege men who moved in an L-shaped fashion? Did pugs dance diagonally? Did a palooka inch along, square by square, like a pawn? And when they got there, to that sweet spot of the board, were they transformed into knights and bishops or whatever they wanted to be? The horses galloped along at a steady pace and the yellow-orange sky turned into night. Ali adhered to a strict curfew and was asleep in his bed, but all the other stars went ahead and came out anyway, dazzling in their insouciant light. The men kept it up all night. I'd never heard so much trash-talking and truth-telling all mixed up together. The cart just kept on rolling down the hill, into the valley and then confidently into the dark beyond. Only Mr. Widdicombe and I did no talking or maybe it was only me, listening and learning and maybe sleeping a little.

♥

Daddy spent most of his day hanging out with Ali and his trainers. Ali followed a strict regimen of morning runs and afternoon sparring sessions; in the evenings he studied films of past and current boxers. Daddy followed the team around with a deck of cards and a pocketful of tricks, ready to perform close-up magic at a moment's notice. Officially, he was supposed to be teaching Ali magic, but mostly he performed.

When I wasn't riding ponies, I spent my time wandering around the camp. On the far side of the parking lot there was a long slope of boulders. Each of them bore the hand-painted name of a famous boxer: Jack Johnson, Floyd Patterson, Jack Dempsey, Rocky Marciano, Sonny Liston, Joe Frazier, Sugar Ray, Joe Louis. Bored, I sat on each of the boulders, pretending that I was interviewing the man whose name was written on the rock.

"Ladies and gentlemen, Rocky Marciano!"

"This fellow here is one of *The Tonight Show*'s favorite people; you know who I mean. I'm talking about Jack Johnson!"

"Sonny Liston, I hear there's someone special in your life these days . . ."

I tried to entertain myself all afternoon, pretending that I was a late-night talk show host and I was interviewing all the greatest boxers who ever lived.

I didn't recognize any of the names except for Sugar Ray, so I wrote the list down and I read it off to Daddy that night in our cabin. He told me that they were great men and that Ali was an even greater man for paying homage to them in such a way.

"A lot of celebrities are so self-involved," Daddy said, as if he hung out with famous people every day. "The thing that sets Ali apart is that he's humble; that comes from Islam. He's also not self-centered; that comes from having a place in history."

"How could you not say he's self-centered?" I asked. "He's always talking about how he's the greatest."

"There's a difference between confidence and ego."

"What's the difference?"

"Ego is when you're all talk. Confidence is when you've got the goods to back it up."

I asked Daddy whether he thought Ali was smart.

"Of course, he's smart. The man's a genius!" Daddy said, looking truly offended at the question.

"Then why is he a boxer? Why isn't he a doctor or a scientist, like George Washington Carver? Why is his job beating people up?"

My father opened his mouth to answer then paused for a second before turning out the light. "I'm going to chalk this one up to you being a girl. Good night, Angela."

♥

Morning was the only time I really got to spend with Ali. Everyone at the training camp ate breakfast together in the dining hall. They gathered at a long wooden table. Ali sat in the center, like Jesus at the last supper.

The first morning, Daddy and I sat in a distant corner, far away from Ali's inner circle. But Ali looked down the table and beckoned me, which meant me and Daddy, closer.

"Come sit by me!" he said. "I love children. They're so pure, so wise. Listen to a child and she'll open up your eyes."

When we showed up for breakfast the second day, two places were set for us across from Ali. We sat there, every morning for a week—front and center with the champ.

"I've got five little girls, pretty just like you," Ali said. "Prettier! 'Cause they look like me."

Everyone at the table chuckled. I melted under Ali's gaze, my heart soggier than the bowl of cornflakes that sat untouched in front of me. I never met Ali's wife, Veronica, but I knew that she lived in California, with her daughters. I imagined her there, passing Mommy on the street, or in the grocery store. I closed my eyes and pictured Mommy repeating what Ali said to me, to one of Ali's daughters, maybe Hana or Laila: "I've got a little girl, just like you."

Ali told my father that he was lucky to only have a girl.

"I love my Angela, but a man always wants a son," my father said.

"What do you need a boy for?" Ali said. "If the king has a prince, then eventually the prince is going to want to be king. He's going to want to whip his daddy. It may not be in the ring, it may be out of the ring, with harsh words and emotions, or it might be worse. Give me a little girl any day. The princess will always love the king, no matter what. Ain't that so, princess?"

I nodded and my father put his arm around me, pulling me in for a squeeze.

"When you grow up, you know what you got to do, Angela?" Ali asked, plowing through a breakfast of steak and eggs and cereal.

When I hesitated, he answered the question for me. "You gotta go to Africa," Ali said. "You'd be a princess in Africa. Marry yourself an African prince and you'd do just fine."

I sat for a moment and thought about it. No grown-up ever suggested that the right answer to "What do you want to do when you grow up?" was "Get married." Lord knows, I'd never imagined myself married to anyone, much less an African prince. But that was the magic of Ali. Everything he said seemed to suggest stepping into a fairy tale. He seemed to believe that your own life story could rival the magic of the Brothers Grimm or Dr. Seuss. After all, he could do it, why couldn't you?

♥

At breakfast on Wednesday, Ali composed a poem for me. He said:

"Angela Davis Brown, with your pretty dark skin.
I told you, go to Africa! Marry you a king.
But first I'll amaze you. I'll pick your card out of the deck.
Ali is a wizard! You never know what I'll do next."

Then he did one of the tricks Daddy taught him. He asked me to pick a card and to show it to everyone at the table. So I did. Jack of spades. I put the card back in the deck and Ali shuffled with as much style as he swung. Ali asked me to cut the deck, then shuffled again. He laid the deck, expectantly, in the middle of the table. He gracefully plucked the top card from the stack and asked me to look at it. "Was this your card?"

He'd found it. The whole table burst into applause. A simple trick, sure, but Ali's first, and mastered in two days. The master boxer proved to be a master student, too.

♥

The next day, at breakfast, Ali did another trick. "You know that I can float," he said. "You know that I can fly. But check me out, I'm a magic man. Pulling quarters from the sky." On that note, he reached behind my ear and pulled out a quarter. Another easy trick, but again the applause was TKO worthy. Then I announced that I had written Ali a poem. This made him smile. "Bring it on, young sister," he said.

"Muhammad Ali! Or should I call you the greatest?
Too early for the paper. Let me tell you the latest.
When I grow up, I'll be a boxer too.
You better watch out. I'll run circles around you!"

Everyone at the table clapped, applauding my audacity more than anything.

Ali just smiled. "Okay, okay. That was pretty good," he said. "But a woman boxer? That's no job for a Nubian princess like you."

"What should she do, Ali?" my father asked mischievously.

"Be a poet! Like Nikki Giovanni," said Ali, after a few moments' consideration. "Or a congresswoman like Shirley Chisholm." It didn't take Ali five minutes to compose another poem for me:

"Angela Davis Brown. Congresswoman from New York State.
Don't forget about Ali, when you legislate.
Take the day I was born and make a stand.
Decree a Muhammad Ali day! Throughout this fine land."

"Will you do that for me, Angela?" Ali asked sincerely, as if I possessed the power to grant him any wish.

"I will. I really will," I whispered.

I pictured myself in a sharp royal blue suit, standing hand on hip, in front of the Lincoln Memorial. I'd seen a picture of Shirley Chisholm, posed just like that, in the *Negro Women of Achievement* book Daddy bought for me. I'd written away for an application to the Holyoke School and I brought it with me to the training camp. Daddy and I did not talk about my actually getting in, but I let my mind spar with the notion and I danced with it around an imaginary ring. Years later, I came to see a connection between my filling out that application and my father signing up for Evelyn Woods's *"Read-ing Dy-namics!"* and the way he made it sound like Jimmy Walker saying *"Dy-no-mite!"* on *Good Times*.

♥

I did not see my father as the greatest that week we spent with Muhammad Ali. I was not thinking about how he planted on my person, like a magician plants an illusion, his staying power, his penchant for self-improvement, his magic. I was too busy falling in love with Ali and walking around the camp in a permanent state of giddy expectation. Six years later, I turned eighteen and read that Muhammad Ali had divorced the beautiful, glamorous Verónica Porche. Just four months later, I read another story. Ali was engaged to marry a woman named Lonnie, a girl who'd first met the champ when she was six years old.

"That could've been me!" I told my father, on the telephone.

"I know, I know," he said, the laughter loud in his voice. "You could've been a contender."

Ali offered me an autographed picture when we left the camp, but I asked him to instead write down the poem he made up for me, the congresswoman poem. He wrote it down and signed it. I held the paper on my left during the full four-hour drive home and was crushed to discover, when I finally let it loose, that I'd smudged the edges with my dirty thumbprints. It didn't matter. When we got home to Brooklyn, I folded the poem up and lovingly added it to my silk scarf of treasures.

♥

Meeting Ali remained the highlight of my father's life. Our week at the training camp was a story he dined out on for years. Even more, all the things my father dreamed of being—a revolutionary, an ambassador to Africa, a great man—took shape when he met Ali. He met the world's greatest boxer not in some fantasy role he imagined, but merely by being himself, Teddo, the Amazing Magician. From that moment on, he thought of his stage name as not mere hyperbole.

Meeting Ali made me stronger too. I don't remember leaving

Deer Park, Pennsylvania, as much as I remember tumbling from that magical place on the hill to our apartment in Brooklyn. Back home, I felt emboldened with a sense of purpose, as if when I closed my eyes at night, I might wake up the next day a congresswoman in Washington, D.C., just because Ali said so.

When Did You Stop Loving Me?

Every Sunday, I have lunch with my father. He takes the train, two hours each way, to Dover Plains in upstate New York, the closest commuter train station to where I live. I've never ridden in with him, but I know my father well enough to know how he passes the time: engaging fellow passengers in either an ad hoc magic show or a rousing political debate—or a little bit of both. Not that he ever cops to it. When the 10:32 Metro-North from Grand Central Station pulls in and my father emerges from the train, I ask him how his ride was. He tells me that it was "quiet," that he "caught up on some reading." But the spine of his book isn't cracked and the departing passengers who wave to him and say, "Have a good weekend, Teddo," hint at a different story. I pick him up at 12:33 and traffic is good. We are home by 1:00 p.m., lunch is on the table by 1:15 p.m.

Over the years, I've picked up my own trove of "boyfriend recipes," though I am careful not to tell my father the stories behind the meals I serve him. Today's is courtesy of Patrick, a British boyfriend my father never met. Lunch is onion pie with a parmesan dough crust, served with a side of roasted carrots and brussels sprouts. "I grew the onions and carrots myself," I tell my father, pointing to the small vegetable garden down the hill from the house. "Oh, honey," he says, rubbing my shoulder with the kind of pity usually reserved for spinster aunts who live with too many cats. "A beautiful woman like you shouldn't have to grow vegetables." I open a bottle of red wine and pour him a glass. "A black woman has to know how to stand on her own two feet," I say, puffing out my chest. "You taught me that."

We follow lunch with an afternoon walk through the woods. There are ten acres on this lot and although I do not own a dog, we can usually count on the neighbor's yellow Lab, Cava, to complete our party. My father sits on the porch steps lacing up the hiking boots I keep for him at the house. They are an affront to his sartorial nature, but he has ruined enough pairs of shoes in the mud to put them on without too much of a fight. I whistle for Cava and we are off.

My father tells me about his job on the Harlem Revitalization Board. It is good work, well suited to a former magician with revolutionary yearnings. In the ten years since my father began working in community development, Harlem has been transformed. There is a Starbucks in Harlem now, a Body Shop, even a Disney Store. My father finds the fact that I live in Connecticut when you can buy a mocha frappuccino on 125th Street to be a major affront. "I'm making Harlem beautiful for you, baby," is what he says when I call him at work.

But I like the country. I've been here two years. When David Dugan, a partner at my law firm, offered to rent me his house, I was surprised. I'd left a roommate notice on the bulletin board in the seventeenth-floor kitchen, but I didn't think partners read any of the myriad notices advertising used high-end cars for sale and associates looking for places to rest their head. I had just broken up with my boyfriend, a trader at Goldman Sachs, and I needed to get out of the Jersey City loft that he owned. It had been my hope that one of the trust-fund babies I worked with would take pity on me and offer me a room with minimal rent on Park Avenue. David's offer was better.

I knew the house from the Dugans' annual Labor Day barbecue. It was more than a two-hour commute from the city, but it was quite the estate. The back lawn rolled down to a river. There was a heated pool, a basketball court, a guest house, and a porch that wrapped around three quarters of the main house. The idea was that the house would be the Dugan family roost, purchased and remodeled, David explained, after twelve consecutive viewings of *Mr. Blandings Builds His Dream House.* That said, even after installing the pool, a generous master suite with a jacuzzi tub, and heated terra cotta floors in the kitchen and all three of the bathrooms, the house remained nobody's dream but David's. His wife felt isolated in northern Connecticut, especially with David commuting four hours a day, five days a week. His daughter, Emily, age twelve, was way too hip and strange, by country public school standards.

Which is how David came to the arrangement he made with me. My role is part tenant, part caretaker. I vacate the house Thanksgiving week and every year from Memorial Day to Labor Day. I pay a minimal eight hundred dollars a month in rent, six hundred in November when I am evicted for a week; utilities are included. I cannot imagine this makes much of a dent in David's mortgage, but Mr. Dugan gets to keep his dream house, Mrs. Dugan gets to keep her classic-six on Eighty-fifth Street and Central Park West, and I get a three-bedroom, three-bathroom house in the country for the cost of a one-bedroom in Williamsburg. It's an arrangement that suits me.

On Saturday afternoons I go into town to do my shopping. There are few enough black women in this town that a flash of melanin across a parking lot, or around the aisle at a grocery store, warrants a second look. I am drawn, as you might imagine, to women my mother's age. She would be fifty-eight years old. She *is* fifty-eight years old. I believe she is alive because I am a probate lawyer and I know that death breaks silences. Wills and burials and hospital bills create trails that reveal connections only the living have the energy and the desire to conceal. Death also has a way of riding the coattails of gossip. We heard, for example, that Aunt Mona's second husband, a man named Eugene, had died; this, although we hadn't seen or heard from Aunt Mona in close to twenty years. News travels.

I presume my mother is alive and I look for her casually, window shopping in the faces of black women I pass in the street. Black suburban women age so well. They are all Diahann Carroll lovely around here—jet black and silver hair, uniformly bobbed by Sarah Jane, the only white stylist in three adjacent counties who can tango with naps. These black affluent women wear color well: their tan and caramel and cocoa skin glistens against their Ralph Lauren reds, Donna Karan blues, and summer whites. And while it is true that good black don't crack, La Prairie works miracles for everybody. I look for my mother among the sepia-toned socialites of Connecticut because I imagine she has done what beautiful women of a certain age so often do—marry well.

I could hire a detective to look for her; there's so much more that I know now than I did when I was eleven. I know her Social Security number. I know the hospital where she was born. I know her blood type. I have even obtained from my father the name of the last dentist she visited, and from this man, her last dental X rays. Sometimes when there is a disaster of national proportion, and it is announced on the news that dental records are being used to identify the bodies of the victims, I sit at the ready. But the trail between us is so cold. When planes explode and earthquakes rumble, nobody calls me. I am beginning to understand that I will hear news of my mother's death, but I won't be summoned to her side, should illness or catastrophe strike. She controls her exits.

I made an extra copy of my mother's dental X rays and I carry them in my purse, in lieu of the wedding picture I treasured as a child. I told myself that the wedding picture was too painful a memory to keep so close at hand. However, if I am honest, I carry a picture of her teeth to remind myself of the pain: of how she bit me and the way she left me to live, part of me breathing, part of me dead. I am a lawyer. I could find her. But I am afraid to look because I am afraid to ask her the only thing I really want to know: when did you stop loving me?

It stands to reason that my mother would tell a different story. Maybe in her world I am an age-enhanced photograph of a missing child, on a flyer mixed in with her newspaper and coupons. Angela Davis Brown. Born: October 1968. Last seen: November

1979 in the Bronx, New York. But I am not missing. I played lacrosse for five years at the Holyoke School in upstate New York. I am five feet ten inches tall. I have dark skin and straight hair, which I sometimes wear, just for fun, in a seventies-style flip. I am thirty-five years old, but I can pass for much younger. Despite the staidness of my profession, I like burgundy lipstick and bright nail polish and heavy French perfume.

When I was a little girl, I got it into my head that when I grew up I was going to be Miss Black America. I went on to become Miss RC Cola, Miss Black New York City, and second runner-up for Miss Black New York. After I graduated from college, I represented the State of California in the Miss Black USA pageant. I keep the sashes and crowns and dried petals of my congratulatory roses in a box, behind my boots, at the bottom of the hall closet. Very few people know about my previous lives as a pageant winner, as a magician's assistant, as the daughter of a great beauty who chose dreams over motherhood. I am a woman with secrets.

Acknowledgments

I am grateful to Paul Hall, John Singleton, and Lise Funder-
burg for encouraging me to start this novel. Jason Clampet,
A. J. Verdelle, and Janet Hill gave me the strength and en-
couragement to finish.

To Caroline and David for providing me with a room of
my own, for my revisions, in their lovely country home.
Thank you. Andrea DiBenedetto's Ferry Road house in Maine
was the sanctuary every writer dreams of: *Grazie*, Andrea.

Huge thank yous to the Council of Humanities at Princeton University for awarding me the Hodder Fellowship. Carol Rigolot, Paul Muldoon, Irene, Cass, Dena, and Matt—I am indebted. I am also grateful to Ruri Kawashima and the Japan Society. I began this novel in Tokyo and while Japan does not appear here, it is, as always, in my heart.

I am grateful for the teaching opportunities that gave me time and space to write and read. I adored my stay at Bowdoin College and am especially grateful to Anthony Walton and Elizabeth Muther for the invite. I am also grateful to the University of Hawaii, Cristina Baccilega, and Mark Heberle for offering me a glimpse of paradise.

Thank you, Sandy Dijkstra, Jill, Babette, Elisabeth, and the entire Dijkstra Agency team. Thank you to Stephen Rubin, Alison Rich, Meredith McGinnis, and the Doubleday family, especially Bill Thomas. Janet Hill's Harlem Moon is the best home a girl could hope for. Thank you, Janet.

Shay Youngblood read early drafts. So did Deb Seager, Saje Mathieu, Matt Dulany, and Jenny Bevill. Judy Ganeles provided invaluable research. Jason Clampet is my IR. Thank you.

Thank you to my twenty-first-century American family, the Ortegas and the Clampets. And many, many pages of love to my amazing nephews, Chookie, Jesse, and Keyshawn and my genius nieces, Sinaya, Magda, and Sophia. May you always remember the wisdom of Baldwin: your crown was bought and paid for a long time ago. All you have to do is wear it.

1. Angela links Melanie's abandonment with Assata Shakur's prison break. How are the two women similar? How are they different? Is there anything revolutionary about either woman's desire and means of escaping the restraints that hold them back?

2. In the first year of Melanie's absence several historical events occur. Discuss how these cultural reference points influence how Angela deals with her mother's abandonment. Do they help her grieve? Hinder that process? Both?

3. Melanie talks about the legacy of the women in her family. How does her abandonment of Angela and Teddo echo her family's history? How does it stand in contrast to what the Brown women would have done? What does it reflect

about Melanie, Mona, and Angela? Is there strength in the legacy? Fear? Love?

4. There is strong yearning for both the American Dream and the idealistic goals of the Black Movement. How does this cultural conflict play itself out in the family? What are the consequences and contradictions that arise from their attempts to attain both dreams? How does Melanie and Teddo's thirst for fame and recognition alienate Angela?

5. Teddo prides himself on being a race man. Discuss how his actions, including his Sammy Davis impression toward the end of the novel, contradict his espoused beliefs.

6. What is the role of magic in the novel? How does illusion and disillusion affect each character? How is magic often linked to freedom?

7. Discuss Angela's encounters with Edward and Sammy. How is her reaction to each of these men shaped by her relationship with Teddo? By the absence of Melanie?

8. Angela and Teddo achieve a small measure of fame and are further rewarded with a week with Muhammad Ali. What is the significance of the boxer in the novel? How does he help Teddo and Angela come to terms with their circumstances? How does he bring them closer together?

9. Teddo eventually finds a way to send Angela to an upstate prep school. Is this also a form of abandonment? A way for him to escape? Is it a way to also free Angela?

10. Angela achieves success as an adult. Discuss her decision not to find Melanie. Has she truly moved on from the memories and desire for her mother? What does her choice of lifestyle and career say about her development without Melanie? With Teddo?